Out of Order

Robin Stevenson

ORCA BOOK PUBLISHERS

Library and Archives Canada Cataloguing in Publication

Stevenson, Robin H. (Robin Hjørdis), 1968-
Out of order / written by Robin Stevenson.

ISBN 978-1-55143-693-7

I. Title.

PS8637.T487O98 2007   jC813'.6   C2007-902771-7

First published in the United States, 2007

Library of Congress Control Number: 2007927584

Summary: Sophie sees her move to Victoria as a chance to start over
and leave her old self behind.

Orca Book Publishers gratefully acknowledges the support for its publishing programs
provided by the following agencies: the Government of Canada through the Book
Publishing Industry Development Program and the Canada Council for the Arts,
and the Province of British Columbia through the BC Arts Council
and the Book Publishing Tax Credit.

Cover and text design by Teresa Bubela
Cover artwork by Margaret Lee
Author photo by David Lowes

ORCA BOOK PUBLISHERS   ORCA BOOK PUBLISHERS
PO Box 5626, STN. B   PO Box 468
VICTORIA, BC CANADA   CUSTER, WA USA
V8R 6S4   98240-0468

www.orcabook.com
Printed and bound in Canada.
Printed on 100% PCW paper.
11 10 09 08 • 5 4 3 2

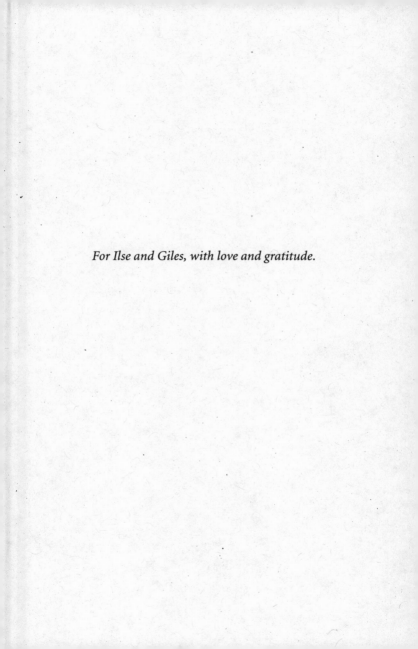

For Ilse and Giles, with love and gratitude.

Acknowledgments

THANK YOU TO Maggie, Ramona, Lynne, Barb and Bird for reading and sharing their thoughts on various versions of this story. Thanks especially to Pat Schmatz, who first read it as a short story, who kept on reading as it grew into a novel, and whose insightful comments and questions helped it take shape. Thanks to Sarah Harvey and to everyone at Orca Books for being such a pleasure to work with. And most of all, thanks to Cheryl May for making it all possible.

Prologue

TOMORROW WILL BE my first day at my new school. Tomorrow will be the test. No one in Victoria knows what I was like before. This is the way I want it. Maybe, if no one ever finds out about the things that happened in Ontario, I will be able to forget about them myself. Maybe the memories will become nothing more than ghosts drifting down the locker-lined halls of Georgetown Middle School.

Keltie shies, dancing sideways, frightened by something only she can see. I sink my weight into the saddle and steady her with my hands and legs. "Easy, girl," I whisper, and she settles and drops back into a trot. I run my hand over the wet silk of her neck. The leather reins are slippery between my fingers.

My face is wet from the rain, but the water trickling across my lips tastes of salt, and I realize I am crying. I shift forward slightly and open my fingers on the reins, letting Keltie increase her pace as we disappear into the trees. The sodden leaves muffle the sound of her hooves. Out here in the woods, I feel safe.

TWO HOURS LATER, we are back at the barn. My legs feel like jelly, and steam is rising from Keltie's black coat. I rub her dry with a rough towel and breathe in the rich smells of fresh hay and sweet feed. As I muck out her stall, pitchforking manure into the wheelbarrow, I feel a calm resolve. I have starved myself all summer; no one could call me fat now. I have been watching the popular kids. I know what music to listen to, what clothes to wear, how to act. I will go to my new school tomorrow, and I will act friendly but cool and nonchalant, like I don't care what anyone thinks. I will leave that scared fat girl behind in Ontario.

THAT NIGHT I lay out my clothes for the morning and go to bed early. My room is cold but I fold my covers to one side and lie still and naked under a single cotton sheet. I reach to turn out the light, and breathe in the darkness. I rest my hands against my belly—hollow, concave, suspended tautly between the sharp bones of my hips. My hands slide up to my ribs—hard fragile ridges. My fingertips dig in, hard, under the bottom edge, feeling the bone from all sides. I trace the scalloped edges of the small hard hollow between my breasts, move up to the lateral tiger stripes of bones running across my chest and then to my collarbones, long and knobby-ended. My cold fingertips graze my shoulders, and my fingers curve behind to find the square bluntness, the corners, the delicate bones at the back that feel like the place where wings should grow.

One

AS I WALK up the concrete steps and through the front doors of the school, my heart hammers out a panicky beat. I keep my eyes straight ahead and tell myself that no one is noticing me. No one here knows I am the girl to pick on. No one can read my thoughts.

Somehow I make it to my first class. English. I take a desk, as planned, in the back third of the room. Not too near the front, as I don't want to look like a keener, but not in the back row, like I'm trying to hide. The seat I choose is next to a couple of blond girls with expensive highlights and tight low-rise jeans. The kind of girls I always tried to avoid at my old school. They break off their conversation and look up.

"Hey," I say. I have practiced this moment in front of the mirror a thousand times.

One of the girls gives me a warm uncomplicated smile. "Hi. You're new here, aren't you?"

I smile back, careful not to overdo it and seem too eager. "Yeah. I wasn't here for grade nine. I just moved out here from Ontario."

"Cool." She leans back in her chair, crosses her ankles and shakes her head so her long hair fans across her shoulders. "I'm Tammy." She gestures to the other blond girl, who is applying lip-gloss to already shiny lips. "This is Crystal."

Crystal nods and smiles. "Hi."

They seem relaxed and friendly, and they look like they are probably fairly popular, although you can't always tell. "I'm Sophie," I say.

We chat for a couple of minutes, and then, to my relief, the teacher arrives and I can relax. For the first time, I really believe that this might work.

Mr. Farley is short and round-bellied, with small wire-framed glasses. He is fairly young for a teacher, and he sits on the edge of his desk instead of standing. He clears his throat several times, and the class gradually falls quiet. "Welcome to grade ten," he begins, his voice surprisingly deep.

The classroom door swings open, and a girl walks in. Black mini-skirt, black leggings, black combat boots. Thick white sweater. Dead-straight black hair that falls halfway down her back. She moves like a dancer.

Mr. Farley stops in mid-sentence, frowning.

The girl slips into a desk in the back row and drops her bag on the floor beside her. I quickly turn and face the front, not wanting to be caught staring.

Mr. Farley clears his throat and resumes his "Welcome to Grade Ten" speech. It's the same one teachers give every year, the one that starts with "This year is an important one..." I try to focus, but all through class I am aware of the girl in the back row. I can feel a tug that is almost physical.

At 9:55 a buzzer sounds and we all scramble out of our desks and funnel into the hallways. Morning break. A whole fifteen minutes to get through before my next class. Tammy and Crystal smile and say they'll see me around. I head to the washroom and lock myself in a cubicle. I read the graffiti. *Jen K is a slut. Mrs. Bardell farts in class. Grady is a faggot.* The usual mindless garbage. But one scrawled line catches my eye. It is written in faded capitals right above the latch: THINGS FALL APART, THE CENTRE CANNOT HOLD. It sounds kind of familiar; I think it might even be from a poem we did in English last year. Still, it sends a shiver down my spine.

I stay in the cubicle until I hear the buzzer that signals the end of break.

THE BLACK-HAIRED girl isn't in my math class, but Tammy and Crystal are. They wave and come to sit beside me.

"So, what do you think so far?" Crystal asks.

"It's school," I say, like this is just what I am used to.

Crystal laughs. "Yeah. Don't you wish it was still summer? The holidays always go way too fast."

Another blond ponytailed girl joins us. Tammy introduces her as Heather. I take this as a good sign. If Tammy and Crystal were a twosome, they might not want me around, but if this is a bigger group, perhaps there will be room for me too.

WHEN THE BELL rings for lunch, the room clears fast. I stay back and follow the last students out the door. I don't want to appear desperate, like I expect the girls to hang out with me. As I head down the hall to my locker, I keep an eye out for them, just in case they ask me to join them.

I check the numbers...462, 464...my locker should be just along here. And then I see her, the girl who came in late this morning. She is leaning against the locker beside mine.

"Hi," I say.

She looks me up and down. My jeans and blue sweater suddenly seem all wrong: babyish, boring, ugly. Her hands are thrust into the deep pockets of an army jacket, and she is wearing no makeup except for dark red lipstick. I wish I looked pale and interesting like her. Even now that I am thin, I have a round face and my cheeks are always pink, like a little kid's.

"Hey," she says at last. "Are you my neighbor?"

I don't get it for a second. My cheeks start to grow warm. Then I realize what she means. "Oh, our lockers...yes. I guess I am."

"It's alphabetical."

I feel like my brain is filled with fog. I can't think clearly, and I take several seconds too long to respond. "Sophie Keller," I say.

She nods and fixes me with the bluest eyes I have ever seen. "Zelia Keenan."

Down the hall, I can see Tammy, Heather and Crystal watching us. I give a little wave, half hoping they won't walk over right away.

They do, though. Tammy smiles, first at me and then at Zelia. "Hey, Zelia, how was your summer?" she says.

"Just peachy." Zelia gives Tammy a big fake smile. "I'll see you around, Sophie." She slings her bag over her shoulder and walks off.

Tammy looks annoyed. "What's with her? Did I say something wrong?"

"No." I shrug. "I don't know."

She exchanges a glance with her friends. "We're going for lunch at the pizza place in the square. Do you want to come?"

It is that easy. I just have to say yes, and I'll be in. I open my mouth to say it, and in that instant I see Zelia standing a little way down the hall, watching. Again, I feel that tug, that almost magnetic pull. I hesitate.

"I mean, if you have other plans…that's cool," Tammy says with a shrug.

"No," I say quickly, pulling my eyes away from Zelia and looking back at the three blond girls. "No plans." I toss my books in my locker and grab my jacket. When I look up, Zelia is gone.

A soft rain is falling as we cross the grass to where the school-grounds back onto a small cobblestoned square. I walked through it on my way to school this morning. At one end sits an old church building with a tall steeple. It is painted in soft yellow and olive green, and a sign out front tells me that it's actually a theater. A long red brick building runs down the other side of the square, housing a weird assortment of businesses: a pizza place, an acupuncturist, a tattoo studio, a hair salon, a gallery.

The pizza place is small and dark, with maybe a dozen tables inside and a couple more outside. It smells of garlic and cheese. I quickly order a coffee and take a table in the back corner while the others cluster around the counter trying to choose between Hawaiian, Greek and Meat Lovers. I am hungry but I feel superstitious; eating anything on this first day might be bad luck.

I couldn't have eaten anything at breakfast if I'd wanted to. My stomach was a tight ache of knots. Mom kept coming into the kitchen to check on me, saying, "Come on, Sophie, just a piece of toast. You have to eat something, honey." I finally told her I had first-day-of-school nerves and she backed off and left me alone. Two minutes later she was back in the kitchen, offering to drive me to school. She seemed so anxious to help that I almost let her. Almost. Arriving at my new school with my mother trying to hold my hand was definitely not part of my plan.

I watch Tammy, Heather and Crystal joking around and giggling as they make their way back to our table carrying slices of pizza on green ceramic plates. Tammy has long wavy hair; the other two have straight hair tied back in bouncy ponytails. All three have long nails, lip-gloss and eyeliner.

I touch my own crazy hair and hope that the rain hasn't wrecked it. It's red, like Mom's, and so thick and curly that it's impossible to do anything with. I spent half an hour with a blow dryer and conditioner this morning, just trying to eliminate the frizz. My nails are short and bitten, but looking at the girls as they sit down, I decide that my makeup is about right.

It's Mom's, but she hardly ever wears makeup, so she won't miss one eyeliner. I waited until I was halfway to school before applying it, bending over and squinting into the side mirror of a parked car. Mom's pretty relaxed—I'm sure she'd let me wear makeup if I wanted to. I just didn't want to have to ask.

Crystal slips into the seat on my left. "So, Tammy says you just moved from Ontario. How come your family decided to live out here?"

I smile and remind myself to meet her gaze. "My gran lives here. My granddad died in the spring, so my mother thought we should be closer..." I trail off, not wanting to talk about myself too much.

She pulls a long stringy piece of cheese off her pizza and wraps it around her finger. "So, are you living with your grandmother then?"

I almost laugh. Having Gran over practically every day is bad enough. "No. No, she has her own place. We're renting a house."

Tammy crosses her legs, jogging the table and slopping a little of my coffee. "I guess you must be missing your friends a lot, hey? I'd hate to move."

Crystal gives a little squeal. "Tammy, you are *so* not allowed to move."

I move my coffee mug around, making wet circles on the table's black surface. "Yeah," I say. "Yeah, I miss them a lot."

Tammy leans across the table toward me, eyes filled with sympathy. "Hey, are you sure you don't want any pizza? It's really good. I'll buy you a piece if you want."

I shake my head. "Thanks. I'm not really hungry."

She takes a bite of hers and chews. "Mmmm. Well, I admire your willpower," she says, her mouth full.

Heather and Crystal nod in unison.

"Yeah," Heather says, "no wonder you're so thin." She puts her hand on her own flat tummy. "I'm totally jealous."

Crystal puts her pizza down. "Me too. I shouldn't even be eating this."

"You all look fine," I say, suddenly feeling irritable. I look past them and out the window. It is raining harder now, fat drops splatting on the tables outside and filling up the ashtrays. Across the square, I can see Zelia. She is sitting on the steps of the theater, smoking a cigarette. She must be soaked, but she looks like she doesn't even notice the rain.

Two

THE FIRST WEEK is a blur of new classes, new teachers, new faces and new names. I learn my way around the school and figure out which, if any, classes I will actually have to work in. Schoolwork is always pretty easy for me. The challenge will be to act the part of the new Sophie Keller. Not to slip up. Not to let anything about the past slip out. I spend my lunch hours with Tammy, Heather and Crystal, who treat me like I've been part of their circle forever.

On Thursday afternoon the sun finally breaks through the clouds. Mom drives me out to the barn after school, and I ride Keltie. We can't ride in the field when the ground is this wet, so we head down the road and onto the trails that circle Elk Lake. It's beautiful, the sunlight sparkling on the wet trees and the rippled surface of the water, but I feel tired and somehow restless. It's weird. Everything is going exactly as I had planned—better than I had hoped even—but it doesn't feel the way I thought it would.

When Mom picks me up, she tells me that Gran is coming over for dinner. I stare out the car window. Gran. I had only met her a few times before we moved out here. When we first arrived, she gave me this amazing quilt she made—a thousand tiny pieces of fabric carefully stitched together, the colors soft and glowing. There was a card attached too, with a note saying she looked forward to getting to know me. She hasn't even tried though; she's too busy looking for things to criticize and complain about. Clearly I am not quite the granddaughter she had in mind. Then again, she isn't the grandmother I would have picked either. I don't know which of us is more disappointed in the other.

Tonight, I have barely pulled my chair up to the table when she starts in on me.

"Riding, were you?" Her eyes are sharp and as brown as chestnuts. "I hope you did your homework first. You don't want to get behind this early in the school year."

I look at Mom, but she just looks away and pretends to adjust the tablecloth.

I sigh. "Gran, if I don't ride right after school, it's too dark. I'll do my homework after dinner." At least I'll have an excuse to leave the table.

She doesn't say anything. She keeps her eyes on mine and shovels a forkful of rice and chicken into her mouth. I always thought old people didn't eat much, but she sure does. She's tiny too. Birdlike.

I take a few bites of chicken and chew as slowly as possible, trying to look like I'm eating more than I am. Mostly I just push the food around on my plate and take sips of water.

"Sophie always does very well at school," Mom says.

Gran grunts, like she doesn't believe it. "You're a terrible one for playing with your food," she says to me. "Always fiddling with this and that."

She is talking with her mouth full of food, which I think is much worse manners than playing with it, but I don't say anything.

Mom catches my eye in a silent apology and turns to Gran. "Could you pass the pepper, please?" she asks.

I wish she'd tell Gran to leave me alone. I push my chair away from the table. "May I be excused?" I say, looking at Gran pointedly. "I should go up to my room and do my homework."

Gran looks at Mom. A piece of rice is stuck to her lip. "Jeanie, the child has hardly touched her dinner."

Mom stifles a sigh. "Yes, Sophie. You may be excused."

THE NEXT MORNING, it is still cold and dark when I wake. I rub my hands across my face, trying to erase the awful night-long dreams of taunts, mocking laughter and shoves in the hallway. I snuggle under my covers and pull Gran's quilt up over my head.

I thought the dreams would stop if I managed to fit in at my new school, but last night was worse than ever. I can't stand the thought of another day of faking it, another lunch hour listening to Tammy, Heather and Crystal talking about which boys are cute, how hard the homework is, which concert they wish they were going to, which girls have the best clothes.

I drag myself out of bed to shower and dress. I look at

myself in the mirror and have a sudden urge to hurl something heavy at my reflection. I imagine watching it shatter into a thousand tiny pieces. Pieces of pink shirt, almost the same as Heather's. Pieces of blue jeans, identical to Crystal's. I close my eyes for a second. You look like one of the group, I remind myself. This is what you wanted. I blow-dry my wild hair into submission, tie it back in a ponytail and walk slowly to school.

Tammy passes me a note in class, slipping the crumpled paper onto my desk while Mr. Farley is writing on the board. I unfold it and hold it under my desk to read. *Are you okay? How come you're so quiet this morning? P.S. I love your hair like that.* Little hearts instead of dots hover over the *i*'s. I look at her and shrug. Then, forcing a smile, I silently mouth that I'm fine.

At morning break, the girls are all extra nice to me. I let them think I'm homesick for Ontario and missing my old friends. The lie hangs between us like a heavy curtain. We have something that looks like friendship, and only I know that it isn't. It's not as bad as being the old Sophie Keller, but it's not much better either.

Somehow I make it through the rest of the morning, doodling tiny screaming faces on the back of Tammy's note— eyes hollow, mouths open in inky anguish. In all my planning, I never thought beyond this point, never planned what to do once I was accepted by the others. It never occurred to me that it wouldn't be enough.

At noon, I toss my books into my locker and slam it shut. I stand there for a moment, facing the closed door. It's the same shade of green as the lockers back at Georgetown Middle School. Everything is rushing at me: the memories of the last two years, Gran's constant criticism, all the lies I have told. It's all swirling around in my head, feeding off itself like wind and fire.

"I think this is yours," a clear voice says from behind me.

I turn around. It's Zelia, holding a piece of paper. I reach out to take it. Tammy's note. Zelia is holding it upside down so the side that we can see is the one covered with dozens of tiny screaming faces. I grab the paper but she doesn't let go. Our eyes meet, and I see a flash of something like recognition flicker across her face.

"Like that, is it?" she says. Her voice is low, amused, sympathetic.

She releases the paper and I crumple it up and shove it into my pocket.

I can't think how to respond, but I don't seem to be able to take my eyes away from hers either.

She gives me a lopsided half-grin, one corner of her mouth curling upwards. "It's Friday."

"Yeah," I say. "But it's only the first week of September."

Zelia's cheeks dimple. "Exactly."

I stare at her.

She shrugs. "It's only the first week of September. Lots of time left to make some changes."

"What makes you think I want changes?" My voice is a little sharper than I mean it to be.

She blinks slowly, blue eyes shuttered. "Whatever." She gestures toward the pocket I shoved the paper into. "Maybe you just like drawing little tortured faces. Whatever floats your boat. Don't let me interfere."

She turns and walks away.

I am still staring after her when Tammy appears beside me. Her constant smile irritates me. It's not fair, I know, but I almost feel angry with her for believing all my lies.

"Hey," she says. "It's Crystal's birthday. We're going for pizza to celebrate."

I look up at her cheerful expectant face. Over her shoulder I can see Zelia, twenty feet away, standing and watching. "You know," I hear myself say, "I'd love to but I didn't bring any money. Another day, maybe." I can hear her saying something about lending me money, but I just smile and shake my head. Then I walk down the hall toward Zelia.

She waits, as if she knew I would follow her. "I had a feeling you wouldn't want to hang out with the Clones for too much longer," she says.

"The Clones?"

"The whole blond American Eagle thing. I can't tell them apart." She shrugs and tosses her head. Her hair is glossy, almost blue black, and so straight and fine that I can see comb lines.

I stifle a guilty laugh. I have been struggling all week not to mix their names up. "They're nice enough," I protest.

She shrugs again. "Whatever." Her eyes meet mine and I hold my breath. With a sudden desperate intensity, I want her to like me. To choose me. But I'm not the type that usually gets chosen.

"I'm going outside for a smoke," she says. She starts to walk away. Then she turns and says over her shoulder, "Come with me?"

"Sure," I say. She walks quickly, ahead of me. I follow her down the hall and out the doors; then I run a few steps to catch up and walk beside her as we cross the grass to the square.

When we get to the stairs leading up to the old theater, Zelia sits down on the bottom step and takes a pack of cigarettes out of her jacket pocket. She waves her hands in front of her, taking in the square in a grand gesture. "Welcome," she says. "I call this place my living room. I try to be on school property as little as possible."

I drop down beside her. It is raining lightly and the steps are wet, the damp seeping into my jeans. A pair of scruffy dogs wander across the cobblestones and sniff through the fallen leaves. I pull the sandwich my mother made out of my pocket, unwrap it and toss it to them. "You don't like this school?"

"This school. Any school." Zelia shrugs and lights her cigarette. "What about you? You're new here, aren't you?"

I nod. "We just moved out from Ontario."

"We?"

"Me and my mom."

Zelia looks interested. "Just you and your mom? Same here. Just the two of us." She flicks the ash off her cigarette, holds it with her hand cupped over it to protect it from the rain. "Where's your dad?"

I study my runners and wish I was wearing boots like Zelia's. "Died when I was a kid, but they split up before I was born, so I never knew him anyway." I turn toward her. "What about yours?"

She leans toward me, ignoring my question. "Aren't you curious about your dad?"

I think about that for a moment, wondering how to answer, wondering how Zelia feels about her own father. I decide to be honest. "Not really. It's always been just the two of us—me and my mom."

Zelia tilts her head to one side as she listens, and her black hair falls over her face. She flips it back over her shoulder with a slender hand. Her nails are short and painted with black polish. "What does your mom do?"

"Psychologist," I say. "Counselling. Our place has an old double garage that's been fixed up. She uses it as an office so she can work from home." I pause. "How about yours?"

Zelia shrugs. "Nothing that interesting."

An old man shuffles through the square and throws us a disapproving look. I drop my eyes, but Zelia just looks right at him and laughs. "Nathan," she says.

"You know him?"

"No, that's just what I call old men."

I grin at her, amused and surprised, forgetting my self-consciousness for a moment. "And what about old women?"

Zelia looks at me, eyes as calm and blue as summer skies. "Why don't you give me a name for them?"

I think for a minute. This feels important, like a test I must pass. "Ethel?" I say, uncertainly. "Or Agatha? Or no, wait...Gertrude?"

Her eyes dance and she claps her hands in delight. "Yes," she says softly, "Gertrude. That is absolutely perfect."

I can feel a huge grin trying to sneak onto my face, but I force myself to shrug nonchalantly. In this moment, I know we are going to be friends.

This is what I believe: that the past will sink like a stone, the cold water quickly closing over it, leaving only a few faint ripples on its glassy surface.

Three

FOR THREE WHOLE weeks, it seems like everything is going to be great. September is almost a perfect month. Sometimes I catch myself smiling as I walk to school, a big goofy grin plastered across my face. Zelia is like no one else I've known. She seems older than the other girls in my classes and more confident. Fearless. She doesn't care what anyone else thinks, and when I'm with her I almost don't care either.

I still talk to Tammy and the others once in a while. There was no fight, no big breakup, but we're already growing distant. We're already forgetting that I almost joined their group. I spend every spare minute with Zelia.

Zelia doesn't ask me questions about myself, so I'm not always forced to lie or make up stories about my old school. And even though I would never let her know about who I used to be, she gets who I am, somehow. She recognizes that we're not like the others. I think that's why she likes me. We're on the outside because we want to be, because we don't want to be like everyone else.

Zelia does crazy things all the time, just to make me laugh. Last week we went into the pizza place in the square, and she asked the guy who works there a million questions about how they make the pizza. Weird questions, like whether they use pickle juice in the dough and do they make a pizza with sardines and avocados. Zelia kept a totally straight face and made her eyes all round and innocent. I had to run outside because I was in danger of losing it, but Zelia didn't even crack a smile. The pizza guy just kept answering all her questions. I guess it doesn't hurt that she is totally gorgeous.

Mostly I still can't believe that Zelia has chosen me, Sophie Keller, to be her friend. Best friend, even. Last week after we had laughed until our faces hurt over the pizza place thing, she suddenly grabbed my arm and got all serious. I was frightened for a second, not knowing what was wrong. She just stared at me kind of solemnly with those blue eyes, and then she whispered that we were going to be best friends forever. I whispered it back to her: *best friends forever*.

The last time I had a best friend was in grade seven. Patrice Low. Two weeks into grade eight she dumped me to hang out with Chloe Rankin and the rest of the gang who went on to make my life hell in grades eight and nine. I'm trying to forget those years. It's easier to keep things secret if I pretend they never happened.

Zelia and I have all these private jokes and games we play, like the name game. Nathan and Gertrude were just the beginning. Girls who are all about clothes and shopping are Madisons; fat women are Berthas or Brendas; bimbos are Tiffanys. Uptight older teachers or librarians are Mildreds or Georges. Clones are just Clones.

One day in the second week of school, Zelia decides that losers will be called Ermentrude, after a slightly chubby girl in our class who wears thick glasses and jeans with a really high waist. Zelia pretends to hike her own pants up to her armpits and does Ermentrude impersonations. Zelia's funny, but I have to fake my laughter. It reminds me not to let down my guard, not to let her know anything about who I used to be.

Sometimes I wake up after a bad dream and sit in sweat-soaked and tangled sheets, trying to figure out what is real and what is not, what was then and what is now. Sometimes I dream that Zelia is calling me Ermentrude, saying I'm fat, laughing at me for believing that she really liked me. I have to get up and splash cold water on my face, stare at my gray eyes in the mirror and feel my newly sharp bones to remind myself that I am safe and that everything is different now. Zelia and I are friends.

I ride Keltie after school a couple of times a week, but on the other days Zelia comes home with me. We hang out in my bedroom, which is small and square, with three walls painted white and one deep red. Gran's quilt covers the bed in a pattern of soft greens and blues, and there is a large round mirror above my dresser, its glass half-covered with photographs of horses I've ridden. I have hidden away all the school yearbooks and the photographs of myself from the last couple of years. The books and CD's that line my shelves have been carefully selected to bolster my new image. Any music I am at all unsure about is hidden under the bed, along with a teddy bear I've had since I was a baby and all my poetry books. Still, I am nervous the first few times Zelia comes over. I can't shake my fear that something ugly might sneak out from the past and spoil everything.

The first day of October dawns gray and rainy, but during the afternoon the wind picks up and clears the skies. When I leave school at 3:30, it is cold and bright. I wait in the schoolyard, looking around for Zelia, and my breath forms plumes of mist that hang in front of me. Everything looks sharp and clear, as if the air is thinner than usual. When I look back on this day, I will remember it as the time everything began to fall apart.

Four

ZELIA WANTS TO go to the drugstore on the way back to my place. I know my mother won't like my being home late, but I don't say anything. I walk quickly and hope Zelia won't take too long.

There are some of those gumball-type vending machines just inside the door. Zelia points at one filled with gaudy jewelry.

"Check this out," she says, laughing. She crams in quarter after quarter and hands me the little clear plastic bubbles that spill out of the machine. I pop them open and empty the shiny rings into her cupped hands. They are ultra-tacky, with chunks of glass for stones: blue, red, green.

"Pick one," she says.

They're all a bit too big. I take a gold one with a green stone and slide it onto my thumb.

Zelia slips a matching ring onto her finger and turns her hand toward me, palm out. I hold my hand against hers in a slow-motion high five.

"Best friends forever," Zelia says.

My breath catches in my throat. "Best friends forever," I whisper. In this moment, I am happy.

We try on all the sunglasses from the drugstore racks, making faces and laughing at each other. Zelia perches a pair of reading glasses on the end of her nose.

"Gertrude," I say quickly. I feel a little twinge of discomfort. My grandmother has a pair just like that.

She laughs. "Yup, they're definitely Gertrude glasses. Points for speed." She puts on a pair of pink-rhinestone-studded sunglasses and strikes a pose.

"Tiffany?" I guess.

"Yup. Points for accuracy." She hands me a simple black pair. "Here, try these ones."

I slip them on and look at myself in the small mirror on top of the rack. I look so different with my eyes hidden. Older. More interesting. More like Zelia. The sunglasses make my red hair look kind of dramatic—kind of striking—instead of just out of control.

"You should get those," she says.

I look at the price tag. "Can't. I only have a couple of bucks on me."

Zelia takes them from me, glances quickly around, and then she shoves them in her jacket pocket.

I stare at her.

"Come on," she says, like nothing is wrong. "I need to get mascara."

I follow, my heart pounding. A fragment of memory pokes through, a sharp little ghost. Girls' voices: *Teacher's pet.*

Chickenshit. Think you're something special, don't you, Fatso? I push the voices back beneath the surface, hold them under. I say nothing.

"Here," says Zelia. "I'll just buy this." She pays for her makeup and we head out into the brilliant sunshine. We're only a few steps from the store when Zelia pulls out the sunglasses and hands them to me. "Present for you," she says.

I cram them hastily into my pocket. "Thanks," I say, and together we walk through the quiet streets to my house.

My mother is in the kitchen, reading a magazine while she microwaves a cup of leftover coffee. Her red hair falls loose to her shoulders, and she is wearing a cream silk blouse and beige dress pants. This means she has been seeing clients; when she isn't working she pretty much lives in sweats.

We never hang out at Zelia's place, but I met her mom once when she drove by the school to drop off some things for Zelia. She is stunning, like Zelia, with the same straight black hair and blue eyes. I bet she doesn't even own sweat pants. She pulled up to the curb in a white sports car, and Zelia grabbed my arm, drew me over and introduced me. Her mother smiled, all shiny red lipstick and white teeth, and told me to call her Lee. Then she murmured something about an appointment, handed Zelia a duffel bag and sped off, blowing us a kiss over her shoulder. She reminded me of someone in a movie. Kind of glamorous.

Mom takes her coffee out of the microwave and stirs a spoonful of sugar into it. She doesn't say anything about our being late, but she gives me a look that lets me know she has been waiting for us.

"So how was school?" she asks.

"Fine," I say.

I would rather just go up to my room, but Zelia pulls up a kitchen chair and sits down. She always wants to visit with my mom. At first I thought she was just being polite, but now she and Mom talk all the time.

"Hi, Dr. Keller," Zelia says. "How's it going?"

My mom nods. "Okay. Busy, but a good day." She looks at me sharply. "Are you wearing makeup?"

I have forgotten to wash it off.

She sighs. "It's okay, Sophie. I suppose most girls do at your age."

I nod vaguely and let my mind wander while Zelia and my mom chat away about makeup, clothes and the eighties music Mom listens to. Mom is laughing and telling some story about trying to iron her hair for her prom and accidentally scorching it. If it wasn't for the fact that Mom and I look so much alike, anyone watching would think Zelia was the daughter and I was the friend.

Zelia grabs my arm and leans forward. "Dr. Keller, Sophie and I were wondering. If you aren't seeing clients tonight, could we hang out in your office?"

I blink. She's never mentioned this idea to me.

Mom looks taken aback. "Why can't you hang out in Sophie's room?"

"Oh, if you don't want us to, it's no big deal," Zelia says. "I just thought, you know, if you weren't using it tonight…"

I wonder what she is up to.

Mom frowns. "Well, I suppose that'd be okay."

Zelia flashes her radiant smile. "Thanks."

I follow Zelia through my house, out the back door and down the path to the office. The door is locked and I have to run back into the house for the key.

Mom catches me and puts her hand on my shoulder. "Is everything okay?"

"Everything's fine," I say, surprised.

"I just thought...I don't know." She looks at me hard, lowering eyebrows which, like mine, are so fair you can barely see them. "You would talk to me, wouldn't you? If something was wrong?"

"Sure. But nothing's wrong. Really."

Mom releases my shoulder. "Okay, Sophie."

When I get back to Mom's office, I don't see Zelia. As I stand there, key in my hand, I hear her whisper.

"Sophie, back here."

She is sitting cross-legged on the damp grass behind the office, hidden from my mom's view. Smoke curls up from the cigarette held loosely between her fingers. She holds the pack out toward me. Oddly, in this moment I remember all my mom's talks about peer pressure and how to resist it. But there is no pressure here, no crowd of smokers, no voices urging me to just try it. Zelia doesn't care if I smoke. If I say *no thanks*, like I always have until now, she'll just shrug and put the cigarettes away. So I don't know why, this time, I reach out and take one.

She stretches out her long legs and smoothes the black mini-skirt across her lap. "Sorry to hide on you," she says.

"I was just dying for a smoke." She leans over and lights my cigarette.

I try to inhale and start coughing. My eyes water. "Why?" I say. "Why do you smoke?" To my horror, my voice comes out almost in a wail.

Zelia's eyes narrow and her voice is cold. "It's no big deal, Sophie. You don't have to smoke if you don't want to."

I shrug, blink hard and pull myself together. "I know. I just wondered." I take another drag from the cigarette. This time I am prepared, and I don't cough.

Zelia watches me. She lets smoke drift out of her mouth. As it slowly wafts upward, she inhales it through her nose. French inhaling, she calls it. She tells me that Lee taught her.

When we finish our cigarettes, we go into my mother's office and I flick on the lights. I don't usually come in here. It makes me feel too weird, thinking about all those strangers talking to my mother, telling her their problems. We used to be pretty close, but I never told her about what happened with Patrice, Chloe and the others. I don't know why exactly; I just didn't want to talk about it.

Her office is nice though, small and cozy. The floor is covered with thick gray carpeting, and a large window looks into the garden. The black leather chairs, which are set up facing each other for a therapy session, are big and comfy.

Zelia gets right into it.

"So, Sophie," she says, "tell me about your childhood."

I laugh, still dizzy from smoking. "Well, Dr Keenan, I had an unhappy childhood…" I begin.

"Uh-huh. I see. And what about puberty?"

Zelia loves to embarrass me by saying words like puberty.

"What about it?" I say.

"What were your early adolescent years like?" She strokes an imaginary beard. "When did you begin your menses?"

I know she is just kidding around, but I feel a rising panic. All I can think about is the other girls calling me a fat loser. The words scrawled on my locker. And that day last year in the girl's washroom when Chloe Rankin and her followers all stood around laughing and talking about me while I hid silently in a cubicle. I can still hear Patrice's voice: *God, I can't believe I used to be friends with her. It's so embarrassing.* I feel like these secrets are written on my face, and Zelia will notice my fiery cheeks, my silence.

Zelia laughs. "It is so easy to make you blush, Sophie. Go on, say it. Puberty. Menses. They're just words."

I make a face and toss a magazine at her, feeling sick and weak with relief. She can't read my mind after all.

"Okay," she says abruptly. "Change chairs with me. Your turn to be the shrink."

We switch chairs. I lean back and cross my legs.

"So," I say, "tell me a little about what brings you here today."

Zelia scowls. "My asshole mother has a new boyfriend."

I forget to stay in character. "She does?"

"Michael." Zelia grimaces and adds, in a sarcastic tone, "He's a therapist."

"Really. How did she meet him?"

"She went to see him a couple of times. As a client, I mean."

"No way. Oh my god. That's wrong, you know. Therapists aren't allowed to date their clients." I've heard my mom rant about this subject many times. Then something else hits me. "Wait a minute. Your mom was seeing a therapist? How come?"

"She's always seeing some wacky therapist or psychic healer or whatever. Last year she was into this weird rebirthing thing—always lying in the bathtub and practicing breathing and pretending she was still in the womb or something." Zelia rolls her eyes.

"Wow," I say.

She shrugs. "Yeah, it was pretty weird."

"So…why does she…I mean…"

Zelia makes a face. "I don't know. She just gets depressed sometimes. And she's always been really angry with her parents. They only live a couple of hours away, but we haven't even seen them since I was a little kid." She shrugs again. "I guess we're not good enough for them."

It sounds like she's repeating something she's heard her mother say. "Don't your grandparents even call you or anything?" I ask.

She snorts. "No, apparently they think it's my fault Lee got pregnant and dropped out of university."

"So that's why she sees therapists and all that?" I ask.

She looks at me. "I don't think there's really anything wrong with her," she says. "She just likes to talk about herself."

I'm not sure what to say so I slip back into the safety of the role Zelia has given me. "So, Zelia. You said your mother has a new boyfriend. Tell me more about that."

"She is totally obsessed with this guy. I mean, seriously obsessed. They are all over each other. It's disgusting."

"In front of you?" I ask, fascinated.

"Oh yeah. If I'm there. Believe me, I try not to be. Why do you think I'm at your house so much?"

This stings, but I ignore it. I make an imaginary note on an imaginary notepad. "Have you discussed your feelings about this with your mother?"

Zelia's mouth tightens into a hard line. "No way. I think Lee would rather I just disappeared. I'm in the way in their little love nest."

I have never seen Zelia cry, but her eyes are shiny now.

She flips her hair back and shrugs. "Whatever. I don't care."

WHEN WE GO back into the house, I ask my mom if Zelia can stay for dinner.

"Sure. Of course," she says. "It's just leftovers."

It's always leftovers, it seems to me. I don't know how my mom manages to serve leftovers practically every night. Left over from what?

I'm kind of glad Zelia is staying for dinner. Mom keeps giving me these looks, and I can tell that, if we were alone, she'd be asking all kinds of questions. Plus, she'd make me eat. Zelia provides some distraction, and when Mom gets up to pour her a drink, I manage to scoop half my macaroni and cheese back into the serving bowl.

"So, can I ask you something?" Zelia says as my mom hands her a glass of iced water. "I'm just wondering. Is there a rule against therapists having, you know, relationships? With clients?"

Mom looks surprised. She has changed into her yoga clothes and tied her hair back, and as she answers she twirls her red ponytail between her fingers.

"You mean, intimate relationships? It's generally considered unethical," she says cautiously. "Why do you ask?"

"Lee," Zelia says. "My mother. She's seeing this guy who was her therapist."

"Oh dear. Well."

I can tell that Mom isn't sure how much to say.

Finally she says, "Well, most therapists feel that it's not a good idea. And most professional organizations for therapists state that it's not ethical or appropriate. But it is a complicated issue."

Her voice and expression are calm. You would never guess that she feels extremely strongly about this. I bet she is dying to ask who the guy is.

Zelia looks at her and narrows her eyes. "If I told you who he is, would you report him?"

"Oh, Zelia…You know, I don't think I should get involved in this. It's your mother's business. It doesn't matter what I think." She looks at Zelia with the same expression she gets when she is worried about me. "Is he…is he treating you badly in any way, Zelia?"

"No," Zelia says, "I just don't like him." There is something in her expression that I can't read. "I don't like him and Lee being together."

My mom sighs. "I can't get between you and your mother, but if there is anything you want to talk about, you know I'm here."

Zelia shrugs. "Whatever."

For a moment, Mom looks like she's about to say something; then she just reaches out and refills our water glasses. We sit in silence for a few minutes. Mom is watching me closely and I eat a few bites, hoping to avoid her attention.

"Can I be excused?" I say.

Mom looks at me, looks at my plate and sighs again. "You hardly ate anything."

"I had a big snack after school," I lie. "Zelia and I went to the drugstore, and I ate a bag of chips." I turn to Zelia. "Right?"

Zelia doesn't even blink. "Yeah, that's right," she says. "We split a big bag of Doritos."

WHEN ZELIA HAS gone home, I take the sunglasses out and put them on. I stare at myself in my bedroom mirror. The lenses are small and black enough to make my eyes completely invisible. I don't know this girl, the one staring at me from behind those dark shiny ovals. I don't know her at all.

Five

ZELIA AND I have started hanging out with the other smokers at school, mostly girls from grade eleven. One of them, a girl called Max, looks familiar. It takes me a minute to figure it out—she looks different now, with thick black eyeliner and her hair all spiked—but then I realize I saw her in the summer. She rides a horse out at Keltie's barn.

"Oh yeah," she says. "I remember you. You own that mare—what's her name? Kasey?"

"Keltie. I don't own her though. I just lease."

"Yeah, Keltie. That's right." Max nods and takes a long drag on her cigarette. "Are you still riding?" she asks.

"Yeah. Most days. You?"

"I wish. I don't have a horse either. I was riding a couple of the young ones over the summer, when their owners were away, but I haven't been out to the barn since school started."

"We should ride together sometime," I say. I am surprised by my boldness.

Max raises her straight dark eyebrows and nods. "Yeah. That'd be cool. I know that Lorraine is going away in a couple

of weeks, and she'll be away for most of the fall. I usually ride
Sebastian when she's not around. Or Tavish says I can ride Bug
anytime. Give me your number. I'll call you."

I fumble in my pocket, find an eyeliner Zelia gave me and
scribble my phone number on the inside of a paper match-
book. I can feel Zelia's eyes on me.

"Come on," she says. "We'll be late to class." Her hand, cool
and hard, grips my arm. I hand my number to Max and follow
Zelia back into the school.

ENGLISH IS THE one class that I actually enjoy. Today, though,
I can't concentrate. I keep sneaking glances at Zelia; I can
still feel her hand on my arm. I wonder if she is mad at me.
I rest my chin on my folded hands and press my teeth against
the inside of my lip. I don't know why she is so important
to me, or why I feel myself disappearing when she is not
around.

Mr. Farley has written an Emily Dickinson poem on the
board. I start to read it silently:

> *Besides the Autumn poets sing*
> *A few prosaic days*
> *A little this side of the snow*
> *And that side of the Haze –*

I'm trying to remember exactly what prosaic means—
boring? ordinary?—when Zelia nudges me.

"Just wait," she says, "he's about to ask us to write a poem about the fall. Guaranteed."

I stifle a giggle, relieved. She's not mad. And then, sure enough, Mr. Farley asks us to write a poem about the fall. Zelia nudges me again, but I have to avoid her eyes or I really will start laughing. Prosaic, I think, means the opposite of Zelia. Zelia is decidedly un-prosaic.

After school I suggest that we go to her place. I am curious about Lee and Michael.

Zelia shakes her head. "No, let's go to your place," she says. "Or we could go downtown. Let's go downtown."

"I have to call home and ask," I say.

Zelia rolls her eyes but walks with me to the pay phones. There's no answer, so I leave a message to tell my mother we're going downtown. It won't be okay with her, but what else can I do?

WE SIT ON the sidewalk down by the bookstore on Douglas Street. It's one of those giant chain stores that are exactly the same in every city. We try to go inside to use the washroom, but they have codes on the doors to stop people who aren't customers from using them.

"It is totally about keeping teenagers out," Zelia states, pushing the buttons randomly. "You couldn't get away with treating any other group of people the way we get treated." She spits the words out like they taste bad. "I mean, how do they know we're not customers? It's like we don't even have basic human rights."

"We could look at books for a few minutes and then ask for the code," I say.

Zelia shrugs. "Whatever. They probably still won't let us."

But they do. A tall girl with lank blond hair unlocks the door and lets us in. Zelia leans close to the mirror and re-does her eyeliner while I pee. When I come out of the stall she takes my arm.

"Okay," she says. "Let's go."

Back on the sidewalk, we sit side by side and watch people walk past. They all look busy or stressed.

"They all look boring, too," Zelia says. "Let's never be boring."

I lean against her shoulder and feel the pull of her personality like a powerful magnet. "Okay," I agree. "We will never, never, never be boring. You must tell me immediately if you think I'm in danger of becoming boring."

Zelia grins. "Deal. And you must tell me."

An old man limps past, leaning heavily on a cane. He looks down at us sitting on the sidewalk and smiles.

Zelia makes a face. "Nathan," she says under her breath.

There is an edge of bitterness in her voice, and I look at her quizzically.

She shrugs off my concern. "Let's never get old," she says. "Old is even worse than boring."

"Mmm. Harder to avoid though," I point out.

"Not really," Zelia says. "I'm going to kill myself long before I get all decrepit and boring and ugly."

I lift my head off her shoulder and look at her. "You are not," I say. "You're not going to kill yourself."

Zelia shrugs. "Whatever."

"Seriously. You wouldn't. How would you do it?"

"If I decided to do it, I'd just do it. How isn't the point."

I'm not so sure. I've never considered suicide, even when my life was pretty much hell. Still, I've wondered about it. Who hasn't?

"I don't know," I say. "I've never really thought about it."

She laughs. "How does that rhyme go? Guns aren't legal; nooses give; gas smells terrible; you might as well live."

I stare at her, unsure if I should laugh.

Zelia just shrugs again. "I think there's supposed to be some line in there about razors too," she says.

Six

I INVITE ZELIA back to my place for dinner. She doesn't bother to call her mom.

"Lee won't notice," she says bitterly as we walk home together. "Michael the Unethical Shrink is moving in this week."

"Moving in! That's kind of fast, isn't it?" I can't imagine someone moving in with Mom and me.

"That's Lee," Zelia says. "Fast. Although maybe this is a good thing. They never last long once they move in." She kicks at a rock on the sidewalk. "She'll probably get tired of him soon. She'll start complaining about little things that irritate her. Then he'll be gone."

I don't really know how to respond to this, so we walk on in silence for a few minutes. Mom hasn't dated anyone for ages. She always had lots of friends back in Ontario, and she did go out with a couple of guys when I was younger. She never seems lonely or anything. She works a lot and goes to yoga classes and book groups and stuff like that. I think she just prefers being single.

The leaves are starting to turn yellow and fall from the trees. They crunch under my feet as I scuff my heels along the sidewalk. I'm curious about what Lee's other boyfriends were like, but I don't want to be nosy.

GRAN IS SITTING in the kitchen, a ball of wool beside her and a craft book open on her lap. So far, craft books are the only thing I have ever seen her read. She comes over all the time. It's been six months since Granddad died, but Gran's still not used to living on her own yet, I guess. Mom says she cries a lot, but whenever I see her, she's as hard and as sharp as the knitting needles clicking away in her hands.

She glares up at me when I walk in arm in arm with Zelia. "A little late, aren't you?"

"I called," I say defensively.

Mom steps in. "It's fine," she says, giving Gran a warning look.

"Look at you," Gran says to me. "You're getting too skinny." She turns to my mother. "Jeanie, look at this girl. She's skin and bones!"

My mom looks at me, and then she turns to Gran, frowning. "Believe me, Mother, I am well aware of it. Just leave her alone, okay?"

Gran raises her invisible eyebrows and says nothing, but I can feel her eyes on me for the whole meal. I force myself to eat a few mouthfuls of salad and some broccoli, but I push the pasta aside. Silently I dare Gran to comment. I know Mom will stand up for me.

Both Gran and I are quiet; as usual, Mom and Zelia do most of the talking. Zelia is telling us about her mom's new job, working for a lawyer.

"Lee says he's the most prominent lawyer in Victoria," she says. "He's really well known. It's a really important position. She's meeting a lot of people."

My mother smiles at her. "That's great, Zelia. I'm so glad things are going well for her."

Zelia frowns and puts her fork down. She is silent for a moment, running her hand through her hair. "She's pretty excited about it. I really hope it works out this time," she says finally.

Gran looks puzzled. "Why on earth wouldn't it?" she asks.

"She's had a lot of bad luck with jobs," Zelia says. She hesitates. "She tends to really like new things, you know? But then after a while she sort of loses interest."

Gran shakes her head disapprovingly.

"Well, maybe this time will be different," Mom says before Gran has a chance to comment. "Maybe she just needs to find something that fits well for her."

Zelia looks down at her plate and nods. "Yeah. Maybe."

AFTER ZELIA AND Gran leave, Mom corners me before I make it up to my room.

"I want to talk to you." She is in the living room, folding laundry. "Here, give me a hand." She hands me a pile of clothes, warm from the dryer. "I hardly see you anymore. Is everything okay?"

"Fine," I say. "I've just been busy. And I have to do homework tonight."

"You were very quiet at dinner," she says.

I shrug. "Gran was getting on my case."

Mom shakes her head slowly. "I know Gran can be critical sometimes—I grew up with her, after all. I know how it feels to have her pick at you. But she's right, you know. You really are getting too thin."

I tense up and brace myself for an argument. "Don't you start too."

"Sophie, I don't want to get into a power struggle with you about this. I can't force you to eat." She takes a deep breath, as if she's trying to stay calm. "I'm going to say this again and I want you to hear it, okay? You are too thin. I'm worried about you."

I drop my armful of laundry on the couch, unfolded. "I think I look fine."

Mom tilts her head to one side and studies my face. "You look beautiful; you always have. But if you keep losing weight, I'm making you an appointment to see a doctor."

I feel myself stiffen. "I'm not even trying to lose weight, okay?"

"Oh, Sophie, please. I see you shoving the food around on your plate, pretending to eat."

I start to cry. I can't help it. "I'm not trying to lose weight, really, Mom. I'm just trying to stay the same, not get fat. You don't want me to get fat again, like I used to be, do you?" Tears clog my throat, but what I feel is anger.

Mom looks like she might cry too. I look away.

When she speaks, her voice is steady. "Sophie, you were never fat."

I stare at the laundry. Blurry scraps of color. I blink, and hot tears spill over and run down my cheeks. I turn away so Mom can't see my face.

She sighs. "You've always been so hard on yourself," she says. She reaches out and puts her hand on my shoulder tentatively. "I don't know why. Am I too critical or something? Do you feel like I expect too much of you?"

"Everything is not always about you, okay?" I shrug her hand off, run up to my room and slam the door behind me.

My eyes fall on the photograph on my dresser. It is a picture of my mother and me at the beach. Her arm is tight around me, pulling me close, and my head rests against her shoulder. The sea is behind us and you can see the white sails flying on the blue water. The sun is on our faces, and we are both laughing.

I remember that moment: it was in August, just a couple of months ago. We'd driven all the way across the country together and couldn't believe we were really living somewhere near a beach. We asked a woman with some small kids to take our picture. I felt like we were on holiday.

I turn the picture to face the wall. Mom and I don't exactly fight, but we don't talk anymore either. It's like there is an ocean between us that gets wider and deeper every day. I wish I could sail across it, but I wouldn't even know how to begin.

Seven

BY MID-OCTOBER, I have a routine that means I'm out of the house as much as possible. On the weekends, after I ride, Zelia and I meet downtown. We always meet in the same place—right outside the bookstore.

Today I arrive first. I sit on the sidewalk, stick my legs out in front of me and tug the hem of my skirt down toward my knees. I have army boots now, like Zelia's. They are heavy and make my legs look really skinny. I cross and uncross my ankles; then I press my boots together so my legs look like they are joined together at the foot, like disposable wooden chopsticks.

A couple of old men are sitting on a sidewalk bench between me and the curb. They are drinking, passing a bottle in a paper bag back and forth. They don't talk or even look at each other.

I study them. The short fat one is a Henry, I decide. The older one, with the beard, is definitely a Nathan.

I slip my hand into my army surplus backpack and feel the cool smoothness of the bottle of vodka I stole from the liquor cabinet at home. My stomach is tight. I promised Zelia I would bring something for us to drink. I haven't ever had more than half a glass of wine, with my mother, but I didn't tell Zelia that.

A middle-aged woman approaches me. She is wearing tight gray track pants, and I can see the line where her hips bulge out above her underwear. A Brenda. I can tell that she doesn't want to get too close to the men on the bench, but she has to step carefully because my legs are blocking the sidewalk. I don't move them: that's against Zelia's ever-growing list of rules.

Of course I don't technically have to play by the rules since Zelia isn't here yet. I'm in our special place though. I'm on our turf. I can feel my skin toughening as I sit here. It's like growing armor, shiny and hard.

Still, I don't let myself meet the fat woman's eyes.

I wonder what Zelia will decide we should do today. I feel a vague apprehension as I lift my eyes and glance down the street. I hate waiting by myself. I pull a pack of Camels out of my jacket pocket, tap one out and light it. I like the rituals of smoking now—matches and Zippo lighters, ashtrays, standing outside with Zelia and the other smokers at school—but the harsh smoke hurts my throat. I only pretend to inhale.

I'm down to the butt when Zelia arrives. She had to have brunch with her mother and Michael, so they are dropping her off. I hastily crush my smoke under my boot heel as the white Mustang pulls up to the curb. Zelia gets out of the car. Lee checks her hair in the rearview mirror and flashes her bleach-bright smile at us as she drives off.

Zelia grabs my arm. "Come on," she says. "Mom made me wear this to the restaurant. I have to get changed." She scowls. "Not like she usually notices what I wear. But all of a sudden I have to dress to impress Michael."

I laugh. Zelia is wearing a pink cashmere turtleneck. She looks like one of the rich kids from school, the ones who spend their winter vacations skiing in Colorado, the ones who drive their own cars and forget their two-hundred-dollar sweaters in the lunchroom.

We repeat our routine of pretending to browse at the bookstore before we get a staff person to let us into the washroom. Zelia yanks her sweater over her head and holds it away from her like it's infested with fleas. She stands there in her bra, pulling clothes out of her bag. When she reaches her arms over her head, I can see her ribs softly outlined under her pale skin. I press my hand against my side, curl my fingers around and count the sharp ridges. It makes me feel safer.

Zelia pulls on a thin black sweater. The sleeves are so long that they cover her hands. Instead of rolling them up, she pokes her thumbs through the wool. It looks kind of like she's wearing gloves with the fingers cut off.

I hand her the bottle and she takes a long gulp of vodka, makes a face, shudders and hands it back to me. I sit on the counter and watch as she takes makeup out of her bag, leans in close to the mirror and runs a black eyeliner along the narrow soft part inside the lashes. Zelia always tells me to put my eyeliner outside the lashes; she says it makes my eyes look bigger. But Zelia's eyes are huge and dark-lashed even without makeup.

I swallow a burning mouthful of vodka and almost immediately feel an answering warmth creep through my arms and chest. I lean my head back against the mirror.

"Do you have the rings?" I ask.

Zelia nods and grins. She roots around in her bag. "Here." She hands me a small velvet bag with a Crown Royal logo.

I slip my hand in, close my fingers on cool metal and pull out our assortment of drugstore rings. I choose a snake with green glass eyes, biting down on its own tail. I slide it on my finger and hold the bag out to Zelia. "Your turn," I say.

Zelia picks out a fat gold ring with a red stone and pushes it onto her thumb.

We take turns picking until we each have three or four rings on each hand and the bag is empty. Then I slide off the counter and stand up. I hold up my hands, palms out, fingers spread. My nails, like Zelia's, are short and painted black. When we run out of black polish, we use permanent markers. Zelia lifts her hands and presses them against mine, fingertip to fingertip.

"Best friends forever," we whisper.

Our eyes meet, and my stomach does a little flip. I look away. Zelia is so beautiful.

We stay in the washroom for a few minutes, sitting on the counter, drinking. I feel a little strange—not drunk exactly, but like nothing is quite real. I get this feeling a lot lately, even when I'm not drinking. It's as if I am remembering a dream. It feels like there is something really important right at the edge of my mind, but I can't quite think what it is. Everything around me looks sharper and brighter and somehow more significant.

I can't explain it to Zelia. I tried before, and she just looked at me like I was crazy, so now I don't say anything.

Finally, Zelia says, "So, I've been thinking about what we should do today."

"Uh-huh," I say.

Zelia starts giggling. She pulls two hats out of her bag and hands one to me.

I pick it up. It is black and old-fashioned, with fake flowers and gauzy bits. It looks like something my grandmother might wear: a Gertrude hat. "No way," I say. "I'm not wearing this, am I?"

"Nope," Zelia says. "Unless you really want to."

I have no idea where she is going with this hat thing, so I take another mouthful of vodka and wait.

"The hats are for money," she says. "We're going to panhandle." She is all excited, looking at me like I'm six and she has just said we're going to the circus.

"What?" I don't get it.

Zelia drums her fingers on her thigh. She is always impatient, always two steps ahead. Sometimes I wonder why she hangs out with me.

"You know. Panhandle. Beg. Sit on the sidewalk and ask for money."

I tug on a lock of my hair and twist it slowly around my finger. "What's the point?" I ask.

Zelia shrugs. "Exactly."

Eight

THE GLARE OF the hazy gray sky hurts my eyes after sitting in the dimly lit washroom. Zelia says they keep the lights low in the washrooms so that junkies won't go there to shoot up. I don't see how she could know something like that, and anyway, the washrooms are always locked. Still, I don't say anything.

We find a spot on the sidewalk, and Zelia arranges us. She is like a stage director, telling me how to sit, where to place my hat, making sure all the details are just the way she wants them. I surrender myself to her sense of purpose.

We sit and wait, not talking. Zelia puts on headphones and turns on her MP3 player. The air is damp and stinks of car exhaust. A woman is walking toward us. Zelia looks at her; then she looks at me. She raises one eyebrow in an unspoken question.

I study the woman. Carefully highlighted hair, pale lipstick, smooth tan. Long legs tightly encased in what Zelia calls spray-on jeans. High-heeled pink sandals cage her feet and shorten her stride.

"An easy one," I say, grinning at Zelia.

She wrinkles her nose. "Yeah. A Tiffany, for sure."

The woman averts her gaze as she approaches us.

Zelia holds out her hat. "Spare any change?" she asks, as if she has done this a thousand times before.

The woman pretends not to hear and walks right past us.

"God," I say. "I'd rather be shot than wear shoes like that."

Zelia shifts to face me. She flips her straight fall of hair back over her shoulder and pulls her headphones off so they hang loosely around her neck. I can feel my own hair curling in the damp air in defiance of the no-frizz leave-in conditioner I always use.

"Next one's yours," she says.

I shrug. "Whatever."

The next person to approach is a woman carrying a baby and pushing a stroller. As she gets closer, I can see that her stroller is full of groceries. The baby is squirming and fussing as she tries to balance him on her hip as she walks.

Zelia nudges me with her elbow, hard.

"Spare change?" I blurt. The woman has already passed us, and I brace myself for Zelia's criticism of my performance. To my surprise, though, the woman stops and turns. She looks at us for a moment and sighs. She is younger than I first thought, and she has shadows under her eyes.

"Sure," she says, "I think I have some change." She shifts her baby onto her other hip, bends over and fumbles in her stroller. A package of diapers tumbles to the sidewalk, and she swears under her breath. The baby starts to cry, a high thin wail.

I find myself mumbling an apology. I get up, step toward her and pick up the diapers.

She finds her wallet and shakes a few quarters into my hat.

My cheeks are burning. "Uh, thanks," I say as I hand her the diaper package.

I watch her walk away. I can feel Zelia glaring at me. "What?" I ask.

"What was she?"

"A Martha," I say.

"Right," says Zelia. "Right. A Martha. Someone who spends her life wiping butts and mushing up carrots. Someone who can pick up her own damn diapers." She is eyeing me suspiciously, as if she can read my treacherous thoughts.

What I'm thinking is: Zelia always goes too far.

Zelia slips her headphones from around her neck and puts her MP3 player in her bag. "You can do the next one too," she says.

It's a challenge, a test. I chew on the inside of my bottom lip. "Okay," I say.

Zelia's mouth is a hard line, her eyes an empty blue.

I wait for the next person to walk past. I'll only look at the shoes, I decide. I'll stare at the sidewalk and I'll only look at the shoes, and when I see shoes, I'll say, "Spare any change?" I'll say it as if I've said it a thousand times before, and I won't look up.

I stare at the sidewalk for what feels like a long time. Pale blades of grass are pushing up through the cracks. Finally I see a pair of feet approaching. Women's shoes. Old lady shoes. A Gertrude, I think. I bite down on my lip nervously, taste metal, suck a fine thread of blood across my tongue.

The shoes are closer now, white orthotic shoes below

bulgy veined ankles. "Spare any change?" I ask. My voice sounds stronger this time, more like Zelia's.

The shoes stop, and there is a long silence.

Slowly, almost against my will, my eyes travel up, past the bulgy ankles, the green floral skirt, the round swell of belly, the cardigan buttoned over sagging breasts. I close my eyes and feel a dizzying rush of shame.

"Young lady," says my grandmother. "What in God's name do you think you are doing?"

I open my mouth, but no words come. A tight lump is swelling in my throat.

My grandmother is shaking her head. "I don't know what to say. Have you been drinking?" She bends closer and I pull back, not wanting her to smell the alcohol on my breath.

"You are completely out of order," she says.

"I—I—It was just a game," I say. *Out of order*. She's right. That's how I feel. Like something within me is broken. I press my hands against my mouth and swallow hard.

She stands still for a moment, her body rigid and unyielding. She looks me straight in the face, and her brown eyes are bruised and bewildered. I stare at her. I stare across the space between us. I can feel my heart pounding at my temples; my face and ears are on fire.

I want to say something. I have a bizarre impulse to jump up and throw my arms around her, but I am frozen to the sidewalk. And then the moment passes. She turns and slowly walks away.

IN BED THAT night I lie awake, wondering if Gran will tell Mom. I pull up my comforter and Gran's quilt, curl onto my side and clutch a pillow to my chest. When I close my eyes, it is Zelia's face I see—her eyes are knowing and blue, and her mouth is twisted in a half smile.

Nine

ON MONDAY, ZELIA doesn't show up at school until after classes are over. She is sitting outside on the steps at 3:30, waiting to talk to me. I want her to ask me how things are going, whether things are okay with my grandmother, but she doesn't.

"My mother is so freaking selfish," she says. "I hate her."

I sit down on the steps beside her. "What's going on?"

"Michael. My mother. She just wants to do this honeymoon thing. I'm in the way." She gives a humorless laugh. "I faked sick so I could stay home today. That really pissed her off."

"You actually look kind of sick. You're really pale."

"Just tired. Can't sleep. I was up all night and just napped a bit this morning. I feel like hell, if you really want to know." Zelia looks at me and scowls. "I suppose you have to be home by four o'clock or something."

I can feel her anger flowing thick and hot beneath the surface of our friendship. She could turn on me in a flash.

"Whatever," I say. I flip my hair out of my eyes carelessly, a gesture I've picked up from her. Then, with something like relief, I remember that I'm riding tonight. My mother will be here any minute to pick me up.

IN THE CAR, I lean my cheek against the cool glass of the window and think about Zelia. She seems so angry sometimes, like she hates everyone and everything, including me. I don't know how she can hold in so much anger. I am afraid it will overflow and come spilling out, scalding everyone around her. I don't want to be standing too close when it happens.

The car pulls to a stop in front of the barn, wheels crunching in the gravel driveway.

Mom loosens her seat belt and twists to face me. "Sophie?"

"What?" It has begun to rain; drops of water tap and splat on the windshield.

"You're very quiet." She hesitates, pressing her fingertips lightly against her lips. "Are you feeling okay?"

I wonder if Gran will tell her today.

"I'm fine," I say. The anger I felt a few days ago has evaporated; the hard shell around me got torn away when Gran saw me panhandling. What do I feel? I don't know. Empty. Apprehensive. Nothing I can explain to my mother.

Mom sighs. "Honey...you don't seem fine. Is school going okay?"

I nod. "Yeah. It's fine. Really, Mom." I put my hand on the door handle.

"I just feel like I never see you anymore. You're never home, and when you are you never come out of your room."

"I'm busy, Mom. I have riding, I want to spend time with Zelia, I have homework to do…That's all." I open my door. "Okay? Quit worrying about me."

She shakes her head and gives a rueful half laugh. "I'm your mother. I'm never going to quit worrying about you."

I slip out of the car. That half laugh means I'm off the hook, for now anyway. "Well, try, okay?" I say. I smile, trying to reassure her. "I really am fine."

I DUCK INTO the barn, out of the rain. Sebastian, the big gray gelding, is standing in cross-ties, freshly groomed. Max's head pops out from behind him.

"Hey," she says, "you riding?"

I nod. "Yeah."

"Cool. Hurry and tack up. I'll wait for you. Want to ride around the lake?"

I nod again. "Yeah. Okay." Max is grinning widely at me, her face alive and happy. I can feel a smile starting to play at the corners of my lips as I groom Keltie.

I slide the bit into the horse's mouth and slip the bridle over her head. Keltie leans into me, trying to rub her big head against my shoulder. I scratch between her ears for a minute before I lift the heavy saddle onto her back.

Max is wrapping blue support bandages around Sebastian's expensive legs. She is wearing black suede chaps over her blue jeans, a black hoodie sweatshirt and a green Gore-Tex jacket. There is no dark makeup around her eyes, but she still looks like herself.

She crams her helmet over spiky, dark brown hair. "Ready when you are."

I tighten Keltie's girth. "Let's go."

A fine light rain, almost a mist, is falling. Everything seems very quiet and still, and we ride in silence for a few minutes. We follow the road for a short distance, and then we cut down a path that leads to the main trail circling the lake. I focus on the rise and fall of Keltie's hooves and the gentle bobbing of her head.

The area around the lake is usually busy with joggers, dog walkers and moms with small kids, but because of the rain, the trail stretches ahead, empty and inviting. I push Keltie into a steady trot, and Max follows a couple of horse-lengths behind.

After a few minutes, she calls out, "Sophie, would Keltie be okay if I brought Sebastian up beside her?"

"Yeah, she's fine." I steady her and slow down to let them catch up.

Max looks over at me and shakes her head ruefully. "He spent a couple of years racing when he was a baby, so he gets a bit silly sometimes if he thinks he's getting left behind."

Sebastian is sweating and tossing his head in excitement. I stroke Keltie's silky neck, and we ride on in a friendly silence, the trail curving along the edge of the flat gray lake. I wonder if Max feels the same sense of peace that I do. I don't know her well enough to ask, and I can't think of any way to say it that doesn't sound stupid.

Around the bend in the trail is a gentle slope, and we let the horses have a good gallop. When we pull up, Max is out of breath.

"Shit. Can we walk a bit?" She shakes her head. "I have got to quit smoking. I can totally feel it, can't you?"

For some reason, I don't feel I need to pretend. "I don't really smoke. I just started, kind of. I just do it sometimes."

"I hate it," Max says, her voice low and intense. "I hate spending money to support tobacco companies. I hate the smell on my clothes and my hair. I hate how hard it is to stop. I hate that I'll probably end up getting cancer or something." She scowls. "I hate everything about it."

"So why do you do it?"

She unzips her jacket. "It's stopped raining." She lifts her face toward the sky for a moment; then she turns back to me and gives a little shrug. "My older brothers smoke, my mom used to smoke. I started when I was eleven. I was too dumb to know any better."

"Are you going to try to quit?"

"Yeah. Again. I'm starting on the patch tomorrow." She holds her reins in one hand and twists her body to face mine. "Don't keep smoking, Sophie. Seriously. You're way too smart to do something that stupid."

Warmth spreads in my belly. She thinks I'm smart, and she says it like it's a good thing. I remember the taunts: *think you're so smart, teacher's pet, brainer girl.* The sting is less sharp though, and instead of the usual instinct to smother the voices, I feel a frightening urge to tell Max about them.

"Let's go. Let's have another gallop," I say, pressing my heels into Keltie's sides. She leaps forward, indignant at my abruptness, and I lift my face into the cool damp air.

Sebastian pulls ahead of us, and Max shouts over her shoulder at me, "Hey! Give us a little warning next time!"

She is half-laughing, and I can see she isn't mad. I grin at her a little wildly and we gallop, hooves pounding the soft dirt trail, until both horses slow on their own, breathing hard.

Back at the barn, we rub our horses dry with empty burlap feed bags that feel rough and scratchy and absorb water well. They smell sweet, like alfalfa and molasses.

A pair of boots and skinny jean-clad legs appear through a hole in the ceiling. Tavish, the guy who helps out at the barn, ignores the ladder resting beside him and jumps lightly onto a bale of hay.

"Hey, Max," he says, grinning at her. He turns to me. "Hi, Sophie. Good ride?"

"A bit wet," Max says, "but good. Are you riding?"

Tavish shakes his head and brushes his streaky brown hair out of his eyes. "No, I've got to pick up a horse from another barn. A new boarder. And I've got a list of chores that should take me until next year."

Max shakes her head in sympathy. "Well, call me if you think you can squeeze a ride in. It'd be good to catch up."

Tavish winks. "Will do." He grabs a long, dark brown rain-coat that is hanging carelessly over a stall door, gives a quick wave and is gone.

"You know him?" I ask Max curiously.

She shrugs. "Sure. We're friends." She picks up a hoof pick and leans against Sebastian's shoulder. "Come on, Seb, pick up your foot." She scrapes the mud from his hoof; then she glances up at me. "So," she asks, "how about you and Zelia? Have you been friends for long?"

I have the feeling she has been waiting to ask me about Zelia, and I feel a little wary. "We met at the beginning of the year," I say. "First week of school. Her locker's beside mine. Keller and Keenan, you know?"

I have no words to explain what Zelia means to me. I'm not sure I even understand it myself.

Max just nods and I wonder what she is thinking. I brush Keltie's mane and tail and paint oil on her hooves and heels to protect them from the fine cracks they sometimes develop in wet weather.

"You want to come over sometime?" Max asks suddenly.

I am startled and pleased. "Sure. Yeah."

"It's a bit crazy, our place," Max says. "My older brothers have moved out, but my mom's remarried and I have twin half-brothers. They're two. It's pretty intense."

"I like kids," I say, stroking Keltie's velvet nose. "I'd love to come over sometime."

Max dumps her brushes into Sebastian's tack box. "I'll call you," she says.

Ten

ZELIA IS NOT at school all week, and no one answers the phone when I call. I eat lunch with Max and her friends, Maisie and Jas. Jas is a tiny South Asian girl with long hair and a loud laugh that contradicts her size. Maisie is her opposite: tall and solid, quiet and fair haired. Despite her constant smoking, she's on the school swim team. They all wear black, and they all pretend not to notice the fact that I throw my lunches, untouched, into the garbage. I drink Diet Coke and listen to them talk, their voices rising and falling in an animated conversation about teachers, boys, music, parents, the weekend's parties.

Max has gone on the patch. She is determined to quit smoking. When we finish eating, Maisie and Jas head to the smoking area, and Max and I walk around, not smoking. Max sucks on mints or chews the end of her pen, and we talk—at first about horses, but gradually about other things too.

Today is Friday and she is celebrating four days nicotine free. We go for a celebratory Diet Coke at the pizza place. It is cool and the air feels damp; we are the only people sitting outside in the tiny, roped-off patio area.

"So where is Zelia? Did you get hold of her?" she asks.

"I don't know. It's weird. She hasn't called me all week. I haven't seen her since Monday. I tried calling about twenty times, but no one ever answers the phone."

Max raises her straight dark eyebrows. "Huh. Maybe they've gone away?"

"She would have told me," I say. "I'd know."

"I hope she's okay," she says.

Her voice is neutral, and I feel like she is just being polite. I think back to when I first met Zelia, and I try to remember my first impression. Confident. Strong. I think that was partly what drew me to her. You couldn't imagine anyone bullying Zelia.

"You don't like her, do you?" I ask.

Max looks uncomfortable. "I don't really know her," she says after a long pause. "You two just seem very...different, that's all."

"What do you mean? Different how?"

Max frowns and fiddles with the ashtray on the table. "Zelia has a hard edge, you know? You seem...softer."

I don't like this. Softer. As in easy to push around? As in fat?

Max is watching my face carefully. "Maybe that's not the right word," she says. "I don't know. Zelia just always seems like she's pissed off about something. Or else she's really insecure. You don't seem like that."

"Zelia's not insecure," I say, surprised. "She's stronger than I am."

Max looks unconvinced. "If you say so," she says. "But you seem pretty strong to me."

A picture of my grade nine self flashes into my mind: hiding in a washroom stall listening to Chloe and the others mock me, terrified that they would guess I was there, crying silently with my hands pressed against my mouth. Voices in my head are whispering *fat cow, fat bitch, fat fat fat.* I wonder how strong Max would think I was if she could see the movies playing in my head.

ON SATURDAY MORNING, the phone rings early, waking me up.

Mom calls to me, "Sophie! It's Zelia. Are you awake?"

"Yeah." I rub my hands across my eyes and sit up, swinging my legs over the side of my bed. I pick up the phone from my nightstand.

"Hello?"

"Hey. So, are we going downtown today or what?"

"Okay," I say, snuggling back under the covers. "After I ride." There is a silence.

"So, are you riding with Max?" Zelia asks.

"Maybe. If she's there."

"Whatever. So, you want to meet downtown this afternoon then?"

I am about to agree. I open my mouth to say *yeah, sure.* Then something heavy shifts and settles inside me. Gran still hasn't told Mom. I haven't talked to her since last Saturday, down on the sidewalk by the bookstore. I don't want to hang around downtown today. I don't want to sit on that sidewalk and mock the people passing by.

I bite my lip, hesitating. "Why don't you come here a bit later?" I say.

It is only after I hang up, still half-asleep, that I realize I forgot to ask where she has been all week.

MAX ISN'T AT the barn, so I ride alone. The sky is a sharp clear blue, and the cold air tastes like burning leaves. When my mom comes to pick me up, Zelia is in the passenger seat.

"I was bored," she says, "so I went round to your place, and your mom said I could come along for the ride."

Zelia makes excuses to hang out with my mom a lot. This is probably paranoid, but sometimes I even wonder if she just wants to be friends with me because she likes my mother so much. I'm always holding my breath when they are together, scared that my mom might say something about what I was like before we came here. In a way, I'm glad I never told Mom about the things that happened at my old school. It makes it easier to keep it a secret.

I rub at a patch of dirt on my hand and watch the fields roll past. I don't know how to talk to Zelia with my mom sitting there beside her. It's like I've split into two people this fall: one for Zelia and one for my mom. The two parts don't fit together, so I just stare silently out the window.

Zelia fills the void, chatting away about nothing in partic- ular. As the fields give way to city streets, she twists around to grin at me and then turns to my mother. "Can I stay for dinner?" she asks.

Mom pauses for a moment before answering. I can tell she wants to say no, but I know she won't. She never does. "Gran is coming over...and a fellow from the university. A colleague. I might do some teaching up there in January." She sighs and shrugs. "Oh sure, stay. The more the merrier, right?"

Gran. I had forgotten that she was coming today. I hadn't realized that I would have to face her tonight. I slouch down in the backseat, glad that Mom can't see my face.

Zelia and I go up to my bedroom. She sits on my bed, leaning back against the pillows. I perch on the end, cross-legged.

"So?" I ask. "Where were you all week? I kept calling."

"Lee kicked me out," Zelia says.

"What? Kicked you out? What do you mean?"

"She wanted to be alone with Michael, so she sent me to stay with my aunt." Zelia grabs one of my pillows and hugs it to her chest. "My freaking old hippy aunt who's stoned half the time."

"Seriously? What did you do?"

Zelia shrugged. "Not much. She lives way out of town, out in Sooke. She doesn't even have a phone or a TV. Mostly I read her weird meditation magazines and tried not to die of boredom."

I can't imagine. "You should have stayed with us," I say.

Zelia brightens. "Really? You think your mom would let me?"

"Of course."

She sighs. "I wish I could live here with you all the time." She stretches her legs out and pulls Gran's quilt over her feet. "So, did you miss me?"

"Of course," I say again.

She looks at me sideways, sliding her eyes toward me without turning her head. "Did you hang out with Max?"

"Yeah. Some." My stomach is starting to hurt.

Zelia's eyes are narrowed and her pupils are pinpoints.

"I don't think you should hang out with her," she says.

Her words hit me, sink in and drop into my belly like cold stones.

I arrange my face to look unconcerned. "Yeah? How come?"

Zelia waves her hands dismissively. "She's a Clone. Just a different kind of Clone. Not like Tammy and those girls, but come on, please. Her and Jas and what's her name, the fat one."

"Maisie," I say, quietly. *The fat one, the fat one.*

"Whatever. They all think they're such individuals because... what? They wear black? They wear weird makeup? It's so lame. They all dress exactly the same and then act like they're so unique."

"They're okay," I say.

Zelia shrugs. "Well, do what you want. Just don't expect me to hang around with the Goth triplets."

I feel like I should say something—argue with her or something—but I don't. I just bite the inside of my lip and feel trapped.

There is a long silence. Zelia opens her purse, pulls out a bottle of black nail polish and starts painting her nails. The smell makes me feel sick.

"Let's go outside," I say.

Gran is standing at the bottom of the stairs; I think she

must have been waiting to catch me alone.

I smile at her tentatively. She ignores my smile and grabs my arm. Hard.

She turns to Zelia. "Go on, you. I want to talk to Sophie."

Zelia looks at me and smirks. I half close my eyes, willing her to leave.

"O-kay," Zelia says. Her voice is low and mocking, but she goes ahead.

Gran holds me away from her and looks at me with eyes like steel. I squirm inwardly.

"I'm really sorry," I whisper. "About last weekend. It was dumb."

She shakes her head. "You know, you're such a lucky girl. You have a mother who loves you, you go to a good school, you have nice clothes, plenty to eat…And there you are, begging on the sidewalk. I don't understand."

"I'm sorry," I say again. "It was just a joke. A stupid game."

Gran snorts. "It's that Zelia," she says. "She's a bad influence on you. I know that type—she thinks nothing can touch her. She thinks she's better than everyone else, but she's nothing special."

"She is better." I feel myself hardening again. "She is special."

Gran shakes her head. "She's trouble, that one."

"I have to go," I say, pulling my arm free. I follow Zelia's path out the back door and to the hidden spot behind my mom's office. Zelia is sitting there, smoking and stripping leaves off the rhododendrons.

She looks at me, eyebrows raised. "Gertrude still pissed about last weekend?"

"Don't call her that." I feel tired. Tired of Gran. Tired of Zelia. Tired of myself.

Zelia shrugs and butts out her cigarette in the grass. "I got some stuff for you. I almost forgot."

She opens her leather backpack and turns it upside down. A cascade of eyeliners, lipsticks, hair gel and jewelry tumbles onto the grass.

I pick up a pair of silver hoop earrings and turn them over in my hand. "For me? How come? Where'd you get all this stuff?" As soon as the words pass my lips, I want to snatch them back.

Zelia's mouth curves in a contented smile. "I missed you, that's how come."

"Well." I chew on the swollen inside of my bottom lip. "Thanks. Can I put it in your bag for now?" I scoop up the pile of stolen treasure. I don't want Mom to see it and ask questions. I don't want to have to lie to her.

I avoid Zelia's eyes. "Dinner's probably just about ready," I tell her. "We'd better go inside."

Zelia uncrosses her legs and stands in one fluid motion, graceful as a dancer. She pops a stick of gum in her mouth and winks at me. "Don't want your mom to know I smoke," she says.

I'm surprised. I didn't think she cared what anyone thought.

In the kitchen, Gran pats my shoulder awkwardly.

"Can I help with anything?" Zelia asks my mom.

Mom shakes her head. "Thanks, Zelia. It's all pretty much ready. Gran's just going to finish setting the table." She casts her eyes around the kitchen. "Here, you can take the salad to the dining room."

Zelia takes the bowl and turns to leave, sniffing the air. "Mmm. It all smells so good, Dr. Keller."

Mom is pulling the lasagna out of the oven. Five hundred calories per serving, I tell myself automatically. Eleven grams of fat. I stare at the lasagna and start to salivate. Okay, you can have some salad, I bargain. My stomach growls.

"Here, Sophie," says Mom. "Would you take the lasagna to the dining room?"

I take the tray and hold it gingerly in both hands. I can almost taste the cheese, the spicy tomato sauce. *Loser. Fatso.* I conjure the memories deliberately, throwing them like darts at the hunger ballooning inside me. What is wrong with me?

Through the open window, I hear tires crunching in the deep gravel of the driveway.

"That must be Patrick," Mom says, rushing off to get the door.

I can hear their voices and laughter in the front hall: Patrick apologizing for being late, and Mom telling him it doesn't matter. Then the kitchen door swings open, and they walk in.

"Sophie, this is Patrick. He teaches at the university. Patrick, this is my daughter, Sophie." Mom looks flustered and anxious.

I put down the lasagna and shake his hand, a little warily. He doesn't look anything like my idea of a university professor. I had expected someone old, maybe balding and wearing glasses, but Patrick looks like he might even be younger than Mom. He has short blond hair and is dressed casually in khaki pants and a cream sweater.

Mom gives me a gentle push. "Let's get dinner on the table. Gran and Zelia are sitting out there waiting. We can all catch up while we eat."

I carry the lasagna into the dining room and sit down beside Zelia. Mom ushers Patrick in and urges everyone to help themselves to food.

Zelia seems to be fascinated by Patrick. She showers him with questions about his work, and he tells us boring stories about meetings at some university in Germany, presentations he has given, dinners with important people in strange cities. Mom rushes around, breathless and somehow out of focus; Gran is half asleep, her head nodding over the bowl of melting ice cream that she didn't want but was given anyway.

Zelia is leaning forward, her fingertips brushing Patrick's sleeve.

"Your job sounds so interesting," she says. "I'd love to travel."

He flashes her a conspiratorial grin. "Where would you like to go?"

"Anywhere. Anywhere," Zelia says fervently. "I've never been farther than Vancouver. I want to go to—oh—Paris. Rome. Mexico. London. And India. Russia. Anywhere." Her eyes are an intense blue, fixed on his face.

"Coffee?" Mom is standing in the doorway.

"Black for me, Jeanie. I'm watching my weight." Patrick winks at Zelia and me as he pats his flat belly.

"I'll clear," I mutter. I pick up my plate of barely touched lasagna, balancing my glass and Gran's bowl in the other hand. As I turn to leave, Mom comes back with Patrick's coffee.

"Could I have some coffee too, Dr. Keller?" Zelia asks.

"I'll get it," I say, leaving the room.

"Black," Zelia calls after me.

In the kitchen, I stare at my reflection in the dark glass of the double-paned window. A double image stares back, one version of my face superimposed on another, not quite aligned. My self and my shadow, split apart. I stand at the sink and drip melted ice cream into my mouth, spoonful after creamy spoonful, until Gran's bowl is empty.

IT IS NOT until later, after Zelia has gone home and I am in bed, that I realize she was flirting with Patrick. She's crazy, I think. She is crazy. He must be at least thirty-five. It's too weird. I mean, he's a friend of my mother's.

I wonder for a minute if I should ask her about it. I picture Zelia pausing in feigned disbelief. She shakes her head. *As if,* she says. *Get serious, Sophie. He's, like, old.* Then she laughs. *You're sick,* she says. *Get your mind out of the gutter.*

But I don't think I imagined it. I doubt she was really interested in him. I think she was just testing her power. I can't imagine anyone being able to say no to Zelia. And I can't imagine how she'll react if someone ever does.

Eleven

THE DAYS SLIP by, getting colder and shorter as we descend into winter. I miss the fall colors I grew up with, the orange and scarlet that brightened the darkening days. Here in Victoria, the rain washes away the color, and the leaves pile up in sodden brown heaps.

I walk a tightrope, riding occasionally with Max and not talking about her when I am with Zelia. Max is a year ahead of us at school, and since she quit smoking and hanging out in the smoking area at school, I rarely see her outside the stables. It makes it easier. She hasn't called me like she said she would, and I am both disappointed and relieved.

Zelia comes over most days after school. Michael has moved in with her and Lee. She talks fast these days, filled with a bright brittle energy. She jumps from one game, one scheme, to the next, taking me along for the ride. She is like a hummingbird, hovering here and there but never landing. I follow her, feeling slow, clumsy and heavy by comparison. Zelia's quick fingers lift money from Lee's purse; they sweep scarves, hats and socks from the shelves at the mall; they wrap themselves tightly through mine as we walk home together after school.

One late November morning, Zelia calls. Her voice is low and rough, like she just woke up.

"Soph, can I sleep over at your place tonight?" she asks.

"Gran's going to be here," I say. What I don't say is that Patrick is coming round to go over some work stuff with my mother. They'll probably meet in her office, but still, I'd rather Zelia wasn't here. Plus, Mom's being a little weird about this meeting. She keeps mentioning it for no apparent reason. I'm starting to wonder if Patrick might be something more than just another colleague. Anyway, I don't much want to be here either.

"You know," I say carefully, "if I came to your place, we could stay out later."

I can hear a smile in Zelia's voice. "True." She draws the word out as if it has two syllables: Tah-rue. "And that chick is having a party. You know. What's her name. One of your Goth triplet friends. Maisie."

"Oh yeah." I wasn't planning to go. Maisie, Max and Jas are a year older than us, and although everyone at school has been talking about this party, I hadn't exactly been invited.

WHEN I SEE Zelia at school she dismisses my concerns.

"It's not that kind of party," she says. "We're not in kindergarten, Sophie. You don't get a little card with a picture of a birthday cake and a note for your mother."

I squirm. "I know, but…"

"So," Zelia says decisively, "we'll go."

ZELIA AND I both have a fifth-period math class but we decide to skip. I rarely skip classes. Not that I think it's wrong or anything, but I'm always scared of getting in trouble. Besides, I actually like math. It's always been easy for me. But I don't want Zelia to think I'm chicken: *chickenshit, chickenshit, fatso's chickenshit*, hisses the voice in my mind. With a surge of anger and defiance I shove the voice away and say, "Sure. Let's skip."

Zelia tells me she has a surprise for me. I follow her across the wet grass of the school fields. We slip through a gap in the fence and drop down a few feet onto the slippery cobblestones of the square.

"We're going to get pizza?" I guess.

Zelia grins. "Nope." She points at the tiny tattoo parlor sandwiched between the coffee shop and art gallery.

"Tattoos? I can't. I mean, I really can't. Mom would kill me."

Zelia laughs scornfully. "You should see your face. You look like a goldfish." She makes a fish mouth at me, opening and shutting her lips. "Don't panic. No tattoos. I think they're tacky anyway."

My ears are burning. I say nothing.

Zelia pulls a fifty-dollar bill out of her pocket and waves it in the air. "We're getting our belly buttons pierced. It's on me."

Inside the door, a few steep steps lead down to a tiny studio. A woman in jeans and a sleeveless shirt is tattooing a man's shoulder. The buzzing of the tattoo gun vibrates inside my chest.

"I'm almost done," she says. She doesn't lift her eyes from the tattoo. "I'll be with you in a minute."

The wall beside us is covered in tattoo designs and photographs of freshly inked arms, legs and backs.

"I'd get this one," Zelia says, pointing at a photo of a woman's arm, the bicep encircled with thin black lines twisted to look like barbed wire. The skin beneath the tattoo is red and swollen.

"You'd have it forever," I say.

Zelia looks at me like I'm completely hopeless. "Duh. That's the whole point."

The woman wipes blood from the man's shoulder and looks up. "Are you girls eighteen?"

"Yeah, we are." Zelia turns to the rack of body jewelry and we pick out our favorites: mine is a thin silver ring, Zelia's a softly curved stainless steel bar that ends in a sparkling blue stone.

"Mom really is going to kill me," I whisper.

Zelia doesn't answer. She picks up a small silver ring. "Maybe I should do something different," she says. "Get my nipple pierced instead."

I wince. "Don't. It'd really hurt. Anyway, no one would see it."

Zelia's eyes are hard, disdainful. "Please. We're not little kids anymore. Besides, who's going to see your navel?"

"That's different," I say, feeling my face get hot. "Anyway,

I want us to both get our belly buttons done. You know. Together."

Zelia grins. "Don't worry," she says. "I was just teasing."

The woman finishes up with her customer, laughing a little at something he says as he hands her a credit card. Finally she turns to us.

"So, you want piercings?"

"Yeah. Navels." Zelia gestures toward me. "Both of us."

The woman looks apologetic. "I'll need to see ID for you both."

Zelia frowns. "I told you, we're eighteen."

"Nothing personal," the woman says. "Just policy. If you're under eighteen, I need your parents here to give consent."

I tug at Zelia's arm. "Forget it. Let's just go."

"It's my goddamn body," Zelia says. "Not my mother's."

The woman shrugs apologetically. "Like I said, it's nothing personal."

"Fuck it." Zelia looks at me. "I'll do it myself."

Twelve

ZELIA LIVES IN a condo down near the Gorge. You can see the waterway from her living room window. I slip my shoes off in the front hall and look around. Thick white carpets, glass coffee tables without a single smudged fingerprint, carefully arranged flowers and knickknacks. It looks like a show home, not a place where people actually live.

I don't know what Lee does exactly, other than that she works for a lawyer. Zelia says she makes plenty of money when she works, but she keeps having problems with her bosses and she changes jobs a lot. They live off credit cards half the time. It makes me uncomfortable when she talks about Lee like this, with a mixture of contempt and admiration.

Tonight the white leather couch is occupied. A dark-haired man in beige cords and a heavy sweater is relaxing into the deep cushions, a mug resting on the coffee table beside him and a magazine open on his lap. He looks up when we walk in.

"Zelia," he says, "how are you? How was school?"

"Hey, Michael. This is my friend Sophie."

Michael smiles. "Sophie, huh? One of my favorite names.

It means wisdom, did you know that?"

I shake my head. "I don't know. I might have heard that before, maybe." He's pretty good-looking for someone that old, and he seems like a nice-enough guy, but I can't help remembering that he was supposed to be Lee's therapist. Not her boyfriend.

"Where's Lee?" Zelia interrupts.

Michael nods toward the door. "Just ran out to get some wine to have with dinner. Should be back any minute." He picks up his magazine in a gesture that is clearly meant to dismiss us.

Zelia ignores this. She drops down on the couch beside him and tucks her feet under her. Michael keeps his eyes on his magazine.

I remain standing, feeling awkward. I have an odd feeling, like I'm not really here or this isn't quite real. The whiteness of the couch, the lazy pose of the man and the beautiful sullen girl beside him—it all looks like a magazine ad or a scene from a movie.

The door opens, and Lee's clear voice breaks the spell.

"Michael?"

Zelia springs to her feet. "Come on. Let's go to my room."

Zelia's room has the same unreal show-home quality as the rest of the house. It looks like a designer's idea of a teenage girl's bedroom. It is entirely too pink and too frilly to belong to Zelia.

Zelia throws herself onto the bed, rolls onto her back and lifts up her shirt. She pinches the skin above her belly button. "I could totally just do it myself."

"Ouch," I say, wincing as I imagine it. "So. I thought you said you hated Michael."

Zelia's eyes are shards of blue glass. "I do hate Michael," she says.

I shrug. "Okay then."

"I'm serious."

"I said okay. So you hate Michael."

She sits up. "Not that, stupid. The belly button. I'm going to do it. Aren't you?"

I hesitate. I like the idea of both of us having pierced navels but…"No," I say.

She jumps up and heads for the door. "Well, you can help me then. Be right back," she says.

A couple of minutes later she returns, holding a glass of ice cubes in one hand and a sewing needle in the other. She places the ice on her bedside table, stretches out on the bed and folds her arms behind her head. Her sleeves ride up her arms slightly, and I glimpse a jagged red cut, partly healed but inflamed and sore-looking, marking the pale underside of her left forearm.

I touch her wrist lightly. "What did you do to yourself?"

She glares at me and yanks the sleeve back down. "Nothing."

I don't say anything. My thoughts are slow and confused, and I find myself remembering a line from one of those books of poems hidden under my bed: *For the eyeing of my scars, there is a charge.* The room suddenly seems too quiet.

"Come on," she says. "Let's do it."

"Are you sure this is a good idea? I mean, it's really going to hurt."

She closes her eyes. "I'm ready."

I lift up her shirt slowly. Then I take an ice cube and hold it against her navel.

She flinches, the skin on her tummy jumping slightly. Then she giggles. "Shit, that's cold."

I giggle nervously too. "That's the general idea."

The ice is melting, and water trickles across her belly and drips onto the pink and white comforter. I reach for a second ice cube but Zelia grabs my arm.

"Enough already. Just do it."

"Me? You want me to do it?"

She grins at me. "Yeah, Sophie. I want you to do it."

I don't want to. Actually, I'm pretty sure this is a really bad idea. "Are you sure?"

She giggles. "Quick, before I chicken out."

I pick up the needle. "Shouldn't we sterilize this or something?"

"It's sterile, okay? Just get on with it."

My hand is shaking slightly. I can hear Lee and Michael's voices from down the hall and wish that Zelia's mom would knock on the door to say hi or to call us for dinner. I wait for a moment, but nothing happens.

"Jesus, Sophie. Get it over with, would you?"

I stare at the needle; then I look at the smooth skin of her belly. "I don't think I can."

"Come on, Sophie. Don't be such a chickenshit."

Chickenshit. I clench my teeth, pinch the fold of skin above her navel and touch the needle to it. It's just a thin fold of skin,

I tell myself. No big deal. The only way to do this, I figure, is fast. My mouth is suddenly dry. I hold my breath for a second and then, feeling slightly sick, punch the needle through as fast and as hard as I can.

"Fuck!" Zelia yells. "Fuck, that hurts." She starts giggling.

I'm laughing too. I can't stop, even though I'm expecting Lee to come flying in any second to ask what is going on.

"Is that it?" Zelia asks. "Is it through?"

I nod. The needle is still sticking out on both sides. I start to slide it out.

"Ow. Ow." Zelia grabs my hand.

"You can't just leave it in there," I point out.

"Let me do it." She grips the needle and, sucking in her breath sharply, pulls it out herself. A thin trickle of blood pools in her navel.

"Now what?" I ask. "You don't have anything to put in the hole."

She props herself up on her elbows. "Do too." Rolling onto her side, she slips one hand into her jeans pocket and pulls out the silver bar with the blue stone—the one she was looking at in the piercing studio. "I figured they owed me," she says.

I feel light-headed and start giggling again. "Well, you can just put that in yourself."

"I intend to." She makes a face at me and laughs. "I sure hope you're not considering a medical career," she says. "Your face has gone totally white."

"Yours isn't looking so good either."

She sucks in her breath sharply as she forces the bar through the new hole. It looks like it hurts—a lot—and I have to turn away.

Finally she is done. "Look at that!" she demands.

The jewelry catches the light from the window, sparkling against the reddened skin. I think of the cut on her wrist and find myself reaching out to touch her belly, just below the blue stone.

"It's beautiful," I say. "It's the same color as your eyes."

Her eyes meet mine for a second. "God, I need a drink."

"Me too. That was the weirdest thing I've ever done."

Zelia rolls her eyes. "Sometimes I think you must have had a very boring life." She pulls her shirt down. "It's a good thing you have me around to keep it interesting."

She slips gingerly off the bed and slides open her mirrored closet door. She has tons of clothes. Lee buys her all kinds of expensive designer stuff that she never wears. Mostly she just wears jeans and funky shirts she buys secondhand.

She strips off her clothes and pulls on a short black skirt, a lacy top and black leggings. Then she slides the closet door closed and checks herself out in the mirror. I look at her reflection and then, despairingly, at my own. Beside Zelia, everything about me is boring. Dull, ordinary, mundane. Prosaic. I ball up my fists and try not to care.

"Is that what you're wearing to Maisie's?" Zelia asks.

I look down at my new black sweater and favorite soft blue jeans. "I guess so."

She sits down, cross-legged, on the floor and starts carefully brushing mascara onto her already dark lashes. I run my hands over my reddish mess of hair, trying to smooth it down. I blow-dried it straight this morning, but it just takes the slightest dampness in the air to start it frizzing and curling again. Zelia doesn't have to do anything to her hair—she quickly runs a brush over it and it's perfect. I scowl at my reflection.

"Borrow something of mine if you want," she says.

"I'm okay with what I have on," I say. At least I'm thinner than she is. I look down at my thighs and note with satisfaction that even these new jeans are fitting loosely now. Zelia is thin enough, but her clothes would be way too big for me.

"Suit yourself," Zelia says, shrugging. "I'm afraid we'll have to sit through dinner with the lovebirds before we can escape." She mimes sticking a finger down her throat and vomiting.

DINNER IS TENSE. It's not because of Lee and Michael though. It's because of Zelia. She has an angry sharp edge tonight, and she and Lee remind me of a pair of cats. They circle around each other's words, wary and suspicious, alternately approaching each other only to leap apart, hissing and showing their claws.

No one cares whether I eat my salmon salad.

The explosion comes just as Lee gets up to fetch another bottle of wine from the fridge.

"Sophie and I are going to a party tonight," Zelia says. Her chin is high, her voice a little too loud. She is not asking for permission.

Lee turns to look at us, tall green bottle in her hand. "What party?"

"A friend's. A girl from school."

"What girl?" Lee's voice is already sharp.

"Just a girl. No one you know." Zelia stares at her mother as though she is daring her to object.

Lee puts the bottle down, frowning. "Are her parents going to be home?"

Zelia stands up. "How the hell should I know?"

Lee turns and looks at Michael. "See what I mean?" she says.

Michael stares at his plate, shifts in his seat and says nothing.

Zelia's face is white with rage. "Quit pretending you give a damn," she says. "You're just trying to do the concerned mother thing to impress Michael. It's such bullshit." She grabs my arm. "Let's get out of here."

I stumble to my feet and glance apologetically at Lee. She isn't looking at us though. Her hand is gripping Michael's arm and her eyes are seeking his.

"Michael, say something," she says.

He is shaking his head. "This is between you and Zelia. I think I should stay out of it."

Zelia stops and turns on him. "A little late for that, Michael," she says.

I follow her from the room. We grab our bags and jackets and head out the door.

Outside it is dark and cold. A light rain is starting to fall.

"Now what?" I ask. "It's too early to go to Maisie's. We could go to my place, I guess. Mom won't let us go to the party though."

Zelia's eyes are shining with unshed tears. "Downtown," she says. Her voice is high and a little wobbly.

We catch the bus and ride silently through the night. Outside, streetlamps and headlights reflect off the wet roads. I have that strange dreamlike feeling again, as if this bus is carrying me out of one world and into another.

Thirteen

THE MALL DOWNTOWN is open so we head inside. It's not even December yet, but the hallways glitter with Christmas decorations, and I can hear a barely recognizable version of "Silent Night." Zelia looks pale under the bright lights, and her mascara has left black smudges under her eyes.

"Are you okay?" I ask, a little tentatively. I half expect her to react with anger.

She sniffs, fumbles in her pocket and pulls out a Kleenex. "Yeah. I guess."

"So…what is going on with you and Lee?"

Zelia shrugs. "I don't know. I'm just so sick of it all. Sick of her pretending shit all the time. Like this important consultant job she has now?" Her fingers scratch the air, making scornful quotation marks around *consultant*. She looks at me and spits out her words. "She's a goddamn secretary."

"So? There's nothing wrong with being a secretary."

"I know. It's just the way she puts out this—this image. And tonight was the concerned mother act. I mean, she hasn't given a damn about anything I've done for years." She stops and stares at our reflection in a mirrored pillar. "I just hate it. I hate her."

I don't know what to say. "Well…maybe she really is concerned, you know? Maybe it's not an act."

Zelia snorts. "Hah. She's been trying to persuade my druggie aunt to let me live with her in Sooke. That's how concerned she is."

"She has?"

"All she cares about is herself," Zelia says. Her voice is icy. "Think about it, Sophie. Did she ask you a single question about yourself? About school? About your family?"

I think about it. She must have. But all I can remember is stories she told about her work, her friends, things she has done and places she has been.

"I can't wait till I can move out," Zelia says. She flips her rain-damp hair off her face and looks at me. "Anyway. Let's get something to drink. For the party."

I laugh. "As if we can pass for nineteen," I say.

Zelia sighs. "You can be so dumb sometimes," she says. "I guess I'd better do it."

She walks away from me, away from the liquor store and toward a guy sitting on one of the metal benches that are scattered throughout the mall. He is maybe twenty—skinny, with a black cap and bad skin. Zelia sits down beside him and says something I can't hear. The guy just laughs and shakes his head. She shrugs, gets up and moves on.

Two women are sitting on the next bench, but Zelia passes them without a second glance. I follow at a distance, watching.

There is a fountain near the elevators, and Zelia perches on its edge. She looks around at the crowds doing their Christmas shopping. After a minute, she stands and saunters over to a middle-aged man with a big belly that hangs over his pants. His arms and legs are weirdly skinny. Zelia places a hand lightly on his sleeve and leans close. They talk for a couple of minutes; then he shrugs and laughs. He takes the money that Zelia holds out to him, and he walks away.

Zelia sits back down by the fountain and looks around. She beckons me to join her.

"Your drinks will be served in a moment," she says.

I gaze into the water. There are hundreds of pennies and a few nickels and dimes resting on the blue-painted bottom. "How do you know he won't just take the money?"

"He won't."

The man goes into the liquor store and comes out a minute later with a brown paper bag.

Zelia takes it from him and he hands her some change.

"Thanks," she says. She grabs my arm and we walk away. When I glance back over my shoulder, the man is still standing there, watching us leave.

Zelia looks back too. "He could be my dad, for all I know," she says.

I turn and stare at her. "What do you mean?"

She doesn't answer right away. When she finally speaks, her words are almost careless but her voice is hard. "I mean, I don't have a clue who my father is. He could be some old pervert."

"But doesn't…I mean…"

She doesn't look at me—just keeps watching the man. "Sometimes I look at men, you know, on buses or downtown or wherever, and I think any one of those men could be my dad and I'd never know it."

I feel a bit lost. "Doesn't Lee know?"

Zelia's face is unreadable. "She won't tell me." She lifts her chin and looks way up at the ceiling, two floors above, as if the answer might be written there. "You know what I thought at school today? I thought Mr. Farley could be my dad. Could be worse, right?"

"I don't think he's old enough," I say. Like that's the point. Then I shake my head. "But why won't she tell you? I don't understand."

She drops her gaze back to my level but doesn't meet my eyes. "She *says* she doesn't know."

"Maybe she really doesn't."

Zelia glares at me. "She must have some idea."

I don't know what to say. I never met my own dad. He and my mom were at university together. I guess their relationship wasn't all that serious, and I was kind of an accident. Anyway, he was out of my mom's life by the time I was born, and he died in a car crash when I was really little. Mom says he was a nice guy and that I have his gray eyes. Sometimes I feel a little sad that I won't ever meet him. And sometimes I wonder if I have a bunch of relatives that I don't know about. I could even have another grandmother somewhere. I asked Mom once, but she said she never met any of his family.

Still, at least I know who my father was.

"Does your mom know that it…that you think about it a lot?" I ask Zelia.

Zelia gives me a look that warns me to back off. "I've told her," she says. She turns away for a moment so I can't see her face. When she turns back to me, her eyes are shiny but a mask has dropped over her face.

THE MALL WILL be closing any minute, so we decide to head to Maisie's party. It is still raining, and the temperature has dropped. Zelia lights two cigarettes and offers me one. For a second, I remember what Max said about smoking. Then I accept it anyway. We smoke with our hands cupped over the cigarettes to keep them from getting soaked.

As we stand at the bus stop, my teeth are chattering. I wore my thin leather jacket instead of a warm coat, and I'm regretting it now. We have poured our vodka into Coke cans, and I take a swig from mine. The alcohol burns a fiery trail to my belly. Cars zip by, spraying us with water from the puddles. So many people with somewhere to go.

BY THE TIME we arrive, the party is well underway, and Zelia and I are already pretty drunk. At least I am, and Zelia must be. She's had a lot more to drink than I have, but she seems exactly like she always does, as if alcohol doesn't affect her at all. I'm feeling kind of light and giggly, not quite in control. Like too many words could easily come spilling out of my mouth.

It feels dangerous, and I have to keep reminding myself to be careful what I say.

Maisie's place is in Oak Bay: a big square house with a huge wraparound porch and a long driveway. Tonight the driveway is crammed full of cars, and music is playing loudly. Some people I recognize from school are sitting outside, smoking, and I can hear Jas's loud laugh.

Zelia's mood seems to improve when she sees the party spilling out onto the porch. She puts her arm around my shoulders and flashes me a quick grin. "Come on, Sophie, let's go have some fun," she says.

We squeeze onto the crowded porch. Jas waves when she sees us and slides over to make room for us on the wooden bench.

"Hey. Cool you guys made it," she says. Her heavily outlined eyes look enormous under her smooth high forehead and neat dark eyebrows. A tiny gold stud twinkles against the side of her nose.

"Smoke?" She holds out a pack, and we each take one.

"So, who all's here?" Zelia asks, looking around. I don't see Maisie or Max. The people on the porch are all grade elevens. I know their names—Keenan, Josh, Ryan, Nicole, Ashlee, Sarah—but I wouldn't expect them to know mine.

"Everyone," Jas says. "Seriously. The house is totally packed. Maisie's freaking out."

"Where are her parents?" I ask.

Jas looks at me and shrugs. "I don't know. Away for the weekend."

A fog is gathering, hanging low and damp over the front yard.

Jas leans back and blows a series of perfect smoke rings into the cold clammy air.

Zelia bends her head close to mine and whispers, "Sophie, what do you think of Josh?"

I glance at Josh. He is sitting on the porch railing, drinking a beer and laughing.

"I don't know," I say. "I don't think I've ever even talked to him."

Zelia rolls her eyes. "Me neither. I mean, do you think he's cute?"

My face feels hot and my mind goes blank. I hate this kind of question. I never know the right way to answer. Back in Georgetown, the girls used to say things like this to torment me. *Sophie, do you think Kevin's cute? 'Cause he thinks you're…uuuhh-gly.*

Once someone wrote on my locker *Sophie Keller is a dyke.* This memory barely surfaces before I push it down. Sometimes I imagine these memories floating under murky water, occasionally surfacing for air. If I can hold them under for long enough, maybe they will drown. Maybe they will slowly sink to the bottom and bury themselves in the silt.

Zelia wasn't waiting for my answer. "I think he is," she is saying. "He's hot. Hey, Jas? Does Josh have a girlfriend?"

Jas points at a blond girl sitting near him. "They used to go out, but I think it's over. He's not seeing anyone, far as I know. Why? You interested?"

Zelia takes a long drag on her cigarette. "Maybe."

"I have to go to the washroom," I say.

When I come back, Zelia is gone. Jas is still sitting outside, blowing smoke rings.

"Where's Zelia?" I ask.

Jas looks at me, her heavy-lidded eyes calm. "She went inside," she says. "Are you okay?"

"Just cold," I say. "I'd better go in too."

The living room is crowded with people I don't know. The music is too loud and I don't know where Zelia has gone. Everyone is standing in tight little groups. I feel conspicuous and awkward standing alone, but I don't know any of these people.

Finally I spot Maisie and some other girls making punch in a huge bowl. A pretty, chubby girl with thick blond hair is pouring a bottle of rum into the mixture. Empty bottles litter the countertop.

Maisie sees me and waves. "Hey! Sophie! Cool that you're here," she says. "Want some punch?"

I accept a glass and move into their circle gratefully.

"Having a good time?" Maisie asks.

I nod. "Uh-huh." The punch tastes terrible, and I down half the glass as quickly as I can. For some reason, I wonder what Mom and Patrick are doing and if their meeting is really a date.

"Where's your sidekick, Sophie?" one of the other girls asks.

I think her name is Mel, and I am surprised that she knows who I am.

"Zelia? I don't know." I don't think Zelia would appreciate

being referred to as my sidekick, and the thought makes me smile. "She sort of disappeared."

Maisie is organizing some kind of drinking game, and I find myself drawn into a circle on the living room floor. My glass keeps being refilled, and everyone is really friendly. I let myself join the laughter as I relax into the warmth of the group.

Someone hands me a pair of dice and tells me to roll them. I don't understand the game at all, but I go along.

"Snake eyes!" someone yells.

"Huh?"

"Double ones," says the guy across from me, taking the dice.

I don't care enough to try to figure it out. I just keep drinking punch, laughing, smiling. Being part of the group.

Someone is passing around a plate of pizza slices. When it is handed to me, I freeze for a second. Then, almost without thinking about it, I grab a slice and start eating. It looks and smells great, but I barely taste it. Even as I stuff it into my mouth, panic is rising like a tide inside me.

"Excuse me," I mutter. I back away from the circle. No one even looks up.

In the bathroom, I bend over the toilet and cram my fingers down my throat. This is the first time I have ever done this. I feel like I should be alarmed by my behavior, but part of me stands separate, observing, and I know that somewhere inside I am still in control. I could stop if I wanted to.

Still, it is harder than I thought it would be. I have to reach my fingers way back, and each painful retch tears at my chest.

I don't think I manage to get rid of it all, but I am sore, dizzy and exhausted when I stop. I look at my pale blotchy face in the mirror and start to cry. I want to go home. I need to find Zelia.

I cup my hands under running water, splash cold water on my eyes and rinse out my mouth. There is some toothpaste on the counter. I squeeze a glob onto my finger and rub it across my teeth.

I look in the mirror again. "You look terrible," I tell my reflection. My voice sounds tinny. I have to find Zelia.

I head down the hall, back to where Maisie was, but she isn't there anymore. Zelia isn't there either. She isn't out on the porch, smoking, and she isn't in the kitchen or the living room.

I go upstairs, pushing past the people sitting on the staircase. A houseplant on the upstairs landing has been knocked over, and I stop to pick it up. Dirt spills onto the pale gray carpet, and I try to scrape it back into the pot.

I hear laughter echoing down the hall. Zelia's laugh. I follow the sound and push open a bedroom door. It is pitch-dark in the room.

"Zelia?" I say, suddenly uncertain.

"Shit," says a male voice. Dark shapes move and shift and there is a crash. The bedside light suddenly illuminates the room.

Zelia and Josh are tangled together on the bed. Josh yanks the covers up to his waist and rubs his hands over his face.

"Shit," he says again. "What'd you turn the light on for?"

Zelia takes her hand off the light switch and sits up. Her boots and most of her clothes are in a heap on the floor.

She is wearing black leggings but nothing else. The blue stone against her belly makes her look even more naked. She's looking right at me with a strange, twisted half smile. I stare back at her and feel numb.

"Sophie," she says, "this isn't really a good time. You're kind of interrupting something here."

"I want to go home," I say. "I want to go home."

She shrugs. "So. Go then."

Hot tears are prickling my eyelids. "Please come with me," I say. "Please."

"What the hell is wrong with her?" Josh mutters under his breath, loud enough for me to hear, even though he isn't talking to me.

Zelia looks at him and laughs. She has this clear laugh that I always thought sounded like water. Tonight it sounds like a thousand shards of glass.

"Sophie, you can go if you want. I'm staying."

I open my mouth to speak, but no words come.

"Go," Zelia says. She reaches out and turns off the light.

I just stand there for a moment, staring into the inky darkness. Then I turn and walk away.

Fourteen

I STUMBLE DOWN the hall. I can't hold back the tears now. I don't care who sees. I sink to the floor, wrap my arms around my knees and cry.

I don't know how much time has passed when a hand tentatively touches mine.

"Sophie? Is that you?"

I look up. It is Max. Her spiky hair is wet, and her eyes are wide and worried.

"Are you okay? No, scratch that. Stupid question." She shakes her head apologetically. "You're not okay. What is it? What's wrong?" Max drops to her knees beside me. "Talk to me, Sophie."

I can't get any words out that make sense. "Zelia," I say. Then, "Gonna be sick."

Max yanks me to my feet and steers me into the washroom. "If you're going to be sick, do it in the toilet, okay?" She turns on the taps and holds a washcloth in the running water. "Been drinking, huh?"

I nod miserably. "Never again."

Max laughs. "Yeah, well, I've heard that one before." She hands me the washcloth. "Here. Wash your face. You'll feel better."

I hold the rough wet fabric against my face and close my eyes. The coolness is kind of soothing. When I was a little kid, I used to get carsick all the time, and Mom always kept wet wipes in the glove box. She'd hand them to me while she drove, folded lengthwise for me to press across my forehead.

"I just want to go home," I say.

She nods. "Okay. I'll drive you."

The cold damp air outside clears my head and settles my uneasy stomach.

"Where were you, anyway?" I ask. "Did you just get here?"

Max makes a face. "Been driving around all night. With my ex. We just broke up."

"Really? I didn't even know you had a boyfriend."

She hesitates. "My ex goes to another school, so you wouldn't know."

I feel a little hurt that I didn't know this. "Well, I'm sorry you broke up, anyway."

Max shrugs. "No, it's okay. I ended it." She pulls her keys out of her jacket pocket. "It was hard though."

"So why did you break up then?"

She looks away. "It's kind of complicated."

We are at her car, a small white Honda Civic. She opens the passenger door. "Hop in, Sophie."

Doing up my seat belt, I feel like a little kid. Too complicated for me to understand—that's what she means. Maybe she's right.

Everything seems too complicated for me lately. I just want to go home and crawl into my own bed.

Then I realize—I can't. Mom would flip out if I came home now, like this. I stare at my hands and start chipping black polish off my thumbnail. "I can't go home," I tell Max.

"What?" Max slips into the driver's seat.

"I'm supposed to be sleeping at Zelia's tonight. Mom doesn't even know about the party."

"Oh." Max looks confused. "So where's Zelia?"

I start to cry again. "In bed with Josh," I say. "Back at the party." I know I shouldn't be telling her this, but I feel hurt and angry. "She didn't want to leave with me."

Max starts the car and turns on the heat. "You're shivering," she says.

There is a silence; then she bangs the palms of her hands against the steering wheel. "I hate that," she says. "It's so lame, the way girls ditch their friends whenever some guy comes along."

"You think she's ditching me?"

Max looks at me seriously. "No," she says, "I didn't mean that. Just, you know, tonight. Leaving you when you're supposed to be going to her place."

I can't stop crying, and my voice comes out in a wail, thick with tears and snot. "What am I going to do?"

Max grabs my hand and squeezes it.

"You're coming to my place," she says.

We drive through the dark deserted streets to Max's house. She presses her finger against her lips as she slips her key into the front-door lock. I tiptoe up the stairs behind her and follow her down the dark hallway to her room.

She pulls the bedroom door closed behind us. "The twins," she whispers. "Mom doesn't mind me being out late, and she won't mind you being here, but if we wake the twins there'll be hell to pay."

I look at her. "Thanks. For letting me come here. Driving and everything."

Max looks surprised. "No, it's fine. You can come here anytime."

She opens her closet, drags a roll of thin foam out from under a pile of clothes and attempts to flatten it on the floor beside her bed. "Will that be okay for you?"

"Yeah, it's fine."

Max rummages in her closet some more and tosses me a sleeping bag. Then she opens a dresser drawer and holds up two pairs of flannel pajamas. "Pink or green?" she asks. "Or you can just sleep in your own clothes, if you'd rather."

I take the pink ones. "Thanks."

We change quickly, not looking at each other, and scramble into our beds. Max pulls up her blankets; then she laughs.

"Forgot to turn out the light." She pads barefoot across the room, flicks the switch and plunges the room into velvety darkness. Her foot brushes my sleeping bag as she steps on the end of my mattress and climbs back into her own bed.

"I'm glad you're here, Sophie," she whispers. "Are you okay?"

"Yeah. Yeah, I am."

The darkness makes me brave, and I ask her, "So how come you never called me? You know, when you said you were going to invite me over?"

Max's reply comes quickly. "I know. I know. I'm sorry." She hesitates before she continues. "You and Zelia just seemed… I don't know. Like you didn't need anyone else. I started thinking, maybe you were just being polite, you know? Like you didn't really want to be friends."

I can feel the blankets shift as she rolls over to face me.

"I wanted you to call," I say. "It's just…it's complicated sometimes. With Zelia."

"Just me being insecure," Max says.

"You never seem insecure," I blurt out.

Max gives a sleepy laugh. "Everyone's insecure," she says. "Everyone."

There is a long silence.

"Max?" I whisper. "You know how I used to live in Ontario? In Georgetown?" My heart is pounding.

I can hear Max's steady breathing.

"Are you awake?" I ask.

Silence.

I wait a moment, and then I whisper my secret into the darkness. "I was kind of a loser," I say. "I used to get bullied. Called names. Stuff like that."

I listen to her breath. In. Out. In. Out.

I match my breathing to hers and slip into an exhausted sleep.

Fifteen

IT IS STILL dark outside when we are woken by the high-pitched shouts and squeals of Max's half-brothers. Light streams in from the brightly lit hall, and I crack my eyes open to see two identical toddlers clad in matching red sleepers. They are bouncing around Max's room, wreaking havoc. One is systematically pulling all the books off the shelves. The other is trying to put my boots onto his tiny feet.

Max pulls a pillow over her head and gives a muffled groan.

I rub my eyes. "Do they do this every morning?"

"Every morning," she says. "It was okay when they were in their crib—I had earplugs—but they learned how to climb out. So now they have regular beds, and they come in here to torture me when they wake up."

"I'd get a lock on my door," I say.

From under her pillow, Max makes a sound that is half laugh, half groan. "Yeah. Somehow I don't think my mother would go for that."

I watch them for a minute. "They are pretty cute, I guess."

"Yeah. Lucky for them," Max says.

I look at my watch. It is six o'clock. Middle of the night. I close my eyes. "How do you do this every day?" I groan.

Max laughs and pulls her head out from under her pillow. "Hungover?"

"Not too bad. Feel a bit sick. If I could just stay in bed…"

She laughs again. "Not a chance, chickie. Come on. You're going to help me feed the little monsters."

"What? Doesn't their mom—I mean your mom—do that?"

"Today's Saturday. My turn to get up early so my mom and Jim can sleep in."

She is grinning.

"You don't mind?" I ask.

"Nah." She laughs. "Well, okay. Sometimes I mind. But not too much."

"O-kay," I say as I sit up. "Ugh."

Max is already up and pulling a sweater over her pj's. Toddler Number Two has succeeded in putting on my boots and is trying to shuffle around the room.

"What are their names?" I ask.

"Caleb and Conor." Max throws me a sweatshirt and a pair of socks. "Catching them is the first challenge. And changing their diapers."

"Oh no," I say firmly. "Oh no. I am not doing that."

Max's brown hair is sticking out in all directions, and she is grinning widely. Her teeth are small, white and very even. "I'll let you off this time," she says, winking. She manages to grab one twin under each arm and hoists them onto her hips.

"Meet me downstairs," she says.

I flop back in the bed. "Sure. Sure."

Zelia pops into my head, but I don't feel as upset as I thought I would. Last night seems a bit unreal.

THE KITCHEN IS painted bright yellow, garish but cheerful. A black and white border collie is bouncing off the walls, chasing the twins, who are squealing with excitement.

Somehow, Max gets the dog fed, both boys strapped firmly into matching high chairs and a pot of coffee brewing. I try to stay out of the way. It isn't until the twins are shoveling Cheerios into their mouths that the chaos subsides enough for Max and me to talk.

"So," Max says. She hands me a steaming mug.

I curl my hands around the warm surface. "So."

"Are you going to call Zelia and find out what happened?" Max asks.

I make a face. "I don't know. Don't really want to know the details."

Max deftly catches a little plastic cup that one of the twins has tossed from his high chair. "Mmm. No. But she must be wondering where you are. I mean, since you were supposed to go to her place."

I remember the fight Zelia had with her mom the night before. "I don't even know if she went home. Anyway, I don't care. If she wants to talk to me, she can call." I push away the mug of coffee. "Can we talk about something else?"

"Sorry," Max says.

There is a moment of awkward silence; then Caleb, or maybe Conor, empties his bowl of Cheerios on the floor.

"More Cheerios," he says happily.

Max shakes her head at him. "Not if you're just going to dump them on the floor," she says.

"More Cheerios," he repeats patiently.

Max sighs. "You won't throw them?"

Caleb or Conor, whichever it is, smiles angelically. "No throw Cheerios."

Max dumps a small handful of Cheerios into his bowl. "Okay, Caleb."

Caleb picks up his bowl, looks at us and immediately turns his bowl upside down. Cheerios scatter and bounce across the floor, and the border collie dashes madly around the kitchen, nails skidding on the ceramic tiles as she chases down every last little piece of cereal.

Max looks at me ruefully. "My cleanup crew," she says.

I laugh.

"So." Max puts down her mug and leans forward. "I'm going out to the barn today. Do you want to ride with me?"

I hesitate.

Max looks right at me and reads my mind. "She'll call," she says softly. "But you can't just wait around."

I nod. "Okay. I'll come with you."

I call my mom and tell her I'm going to the barn with Max. I don't mention that I spent the night at Max's instead of Zelia's, and she doesn't ask too many questions. My mom is kind of strict, but she isn't nosy. I am thinking about Zelia and Lee when Max's mother bounces into the kitchen.

She looks so much like the twins that I almost laugh out loud: white blond hair forming a static halo around her head, a broad grin and a chubby body wrapped in an ancient housecoat the exact same shade of red as the twins' sleepers. I like her instantly.

"Morning, girls," she says, giving Max a kiss on the top of her head. "And boys," she adds, ruffling the twins' hair. "Max, thanks for the sleep-in."

Max looks at her watch. "It's not even seven. Go back to bed, if you want."

Her mom winks. "Jim's snoring loud enough to wake the dead. So I'm up, and you two are officially off duty."

She looks at me for the first time. "I don't think we've met. I'm Georgie."

"Sophie. Hi," I say, feeling a little shy.

"Sophie. Of course. The good rider. Max has talked about you."

I look at Max, surprised, but her face is turned away as she lifts the boys from their high chairs.

"Well," Georgie says, "I'll take these two and let you girls get going. You're heading out to the barn, I take it?"

Max nods. "If we can borrow the car."

"No worries. Pick up milk on your way home. Oh, and lettuce. And bananas for the boys."

IN THE CAR, Max is quiet. She drives the way she does everything else, giving it her full attention. I keep pushing thoughts of Zelia out of my head, especially thoughts of her and Josh together in that dark room. I don't know what I feel. There's a weight in my belly that could be anger, but I think it's mostly fear. I'm scared of losing her. I wish things could go back to the way they were in September: the excitement of a new friendship, the secret thrill of starting over, re-creating myself.

I sneak a glance at Max from the passenger seat. She has a strong face with definite features: dark eyebrows, clear skin, straight nose, square chin with a small dent in its center. So different from Zelia. Max isn't exactly pretty, but I like her face. It suits who she is.

"What?" Max says suddenly.

"Huh?"

"You're staring at me."

I feel my cheeks and ears get warm. I wish I didn't blush so easily.

"Sorry," I say.

"S'okay. I just wondered what you were thinking about."

"Nothing," I say.

Max always seems so confident. Of course, I've always thought that about Zelia too. Maybe I'm the only one who can't just be myself. Whoever that is.

"Hey, Max," I say.

"Mmm?"

"Have you ever had Mr. Delgado for art?"

"No. Why?"

"He said this thing in class last week," I begin. I hope I can explain this properly and that Max doesn't think it's totally dumb. "He said that this sculptor, Michelangelo, believed that statues already existed within the marble, and the sculptor's job was to chip away all the excess stone. You know, to reveal the figure inside."

"Cool." Max looks at me expectantly, like she knows where I'm going with this but wants to hear it anyway.

I bite my lip, hesitating, and then plunge forward. "So I was thinking…what if we're kind of like the statues, you know? Like there is some way we are supposed to be or really are inside…and all this stuff we're doing now is just the way we chip away at the stone. Just living our lives and bumping up against things, knocking bits of stone off here and there…" I hold my breath and scrutinize Max's face for any sign of scorn.

There is a long pause in which Max nods thoughtfully.

"I like it," she says. "Though, I don't know. Do you really think we are supposed to be one particular way?"

She keeps glancing sideways at me while she drives, watching my face for my reaction. As if my answer is really important.

For some reason, a picture of Gran pops into my head: her shocked face when she saw me on the sidewalk that day. I watch the trees flashing past, and I choose my words carefully. "Yeah. I guess it's not a totally rigid thing—I mean, we can change and make choices and all that, as long as we're honest about who we are."

When I finish talking, I look over at Max.

Her cheeks are suddenly flushed, and when she speaks, her voice is forceful, almost angry.

"You can't always be honest about who you are," she says.

There is a long silence. I stare down at my feet, wishing I could snatch back my words although I don't know what I have done wrong.

Max sighs. "Sorry, Sophie. I didn't mean to bite your head off. It's not you."

"What is it? What's wrong?" I whisper.

She shakes her head. "It's nothing. Forget it."

We drive in silence for a few minutes, and then Max starts asking me questions about riding. It is obvious she wants to change the subject, and I chatter on, wanting things to feel normal between us again. Inside, though, I'm dying to know what it is that Max can't say. I'm wondering if her secret is anything like mine.

Sixteen

MAX PARKS NEATLY beside the barn, and we pull on gloves and hats before we even get out of the car. It's cold and clear and the barn smells like apples, sweet feed and leather. Tavish is sitting on a bale of hay, cleaning a saddle.

"Hey, Sophie. Hey, Max," he says. He looks up, and then he quickly drops his eyes back to the saddle. His light brown hair flops forward over his eyes. It reminds me of a horse's forelock.

"You riding today?" he asks, rubbing a sponge against a block of saddle soap.

Max answers. "Yeah. You should ride with us, Tavish."

"Lots to do," he says.

Tavish never says much. I guess some people would think it's weird, the way he never makes small talk, but it's one of the things I like about him. He never talks just for the sake of talking.

Max laughs. "Yeah, and you have to exercise Schooner too…and Honey…and your own horse. So come with us."

Tavish looks at me. "Is that cool?"

"Sure. Of course," I say, surprised. "I mean, that'd be fine. Great."

A quick grin creases his face, lights up his eyes and disappears just as fast as it came. "Okay then. I'll go get Schooner ready." He lifts the saddle and places it gently on the door of an empty stall. Then he disappears down the aisle of the barn.

Max looks at me and winks. "He likes you," she whispers.

"Shhh. He does not," I say immediately. I'm embarrassed but curious. I've never really thought about Tavish much. "Why? I mean, what makes you think so?"

"Obvious."

"Not to me."

"Well…he's all shy around you. He keeps looking at you, then looking away. He practically blushes when you talk to him."

My own cheeks are burning. "Max! Stop it."

Max laughs. "I think it's kind of sweet."

We ride into the woods and follow the wide dirt trail around the edge of the lake. We are quiet, and I keep thinking about what Max said. I wish she hadn't said it. I want to enjoy the silence, feel the rhythm of the hoofbeats, lose myself in Keltie's speed and power. Instead I find myself sneaking glances at Tavish, noticing how his long legs wrap around Schooner's narrow sides, how his gray leather chaps are old and stained with mud. I wonder if Max was just teasing me.

We come to a long gentle slope where we often gallop, and Keltie starts dancing sideways in anticipation. I close my fingers on the reins and sit deeply in the saddle to steady her.

"Easy girl," I murmur.

Max looks over her shoulder at me, eyebrows raised in a silent question.

I look at Tavish. "Would Schooner be okay for a gallop?" I ask. "He's the baby of the group."

Tavish runs a hand down Schooner's hard gray neck. "He'll be fine."

I let Keltie go: relax my hands, lean forward slightly, drop my weight into my heels. She leaps forward, lowering her head and releasing all that pent-up energy in a burst of speed. Hooves drum on the hard ground. Ahead of me, I watch Max fight to keep Sebastian under control; he is shaking his head and it looks like he is trying to buck. A spray of mud from his hooves splatters across my face. I can hear Schooner snorting and pounding behind me. The wind burns my eyes and snatches tears from my cheeks. For a sharp second, I remember Zelia, half-naked and tangled in bed with Josh, but I push the image aside, close my eyes and lose myself in sensation, in speed, in the power singing in my veins.

When we finally pull up, all three horses are breathing hard, and we are all laughing and breathless.

"Did you see Sebastian?" Max slaps his neck affectionately. "Old lunatic nearly bucked me off."

Tavish is grinning widely. "That was great."

He looks at me. His eyes are the color of celery.

"It was great," I say softly. It was better than great; it was like, just for a moment, I'd grown wings. I grin back at him. "It was incredible."

By the time we get back to the barn, the horses are cool but still sweaty. We tie them in the aisle and rub them dry. I toss brushes out of my box but can't find my hoof pick.

"Here," Tavish says, handing me his.

I reach out to take it, and our hands touch for a second. Before, I wouldn't even have noticed this, but now I'm self-conscious and quickly pull my hand away, dropping the pick. I bend over to grab it, and my eyes meet Tavish's.

"You've got mud all over your face, did you know?" he says.

I laugh, relieved. Max must have been imagining things. "Yeah. Thank Sebastian for that." I rub my hands over my face. "Any better?"

"Well…if you consider streaks an improvement on splotches."

"Oh yeah. Definitely. Thanks, Tavish."

Tavish fumbles in a pocket. "I have a rag somewhere. Well, I thought I did." He pulls out a pack of candy instead. "Here. Have a Life Saver."

"No, thanks."

"Come on…they're butterscotch. And you're way too skinny."

Mom and Gran are always saying this, and I usually just tune it out. Now, for some reason, I find myself looking down at my legs. My once-snug riding boots are loose around my calves, and for a second I wonder if Tavish is right. The thought slips like a splinter under my skin, sharp and uncomfortable. I shrug and try to ignore it.

"Not for me, thanks," I say.

He sticks the pack of candy back in his pocket. "Keltie enjoyed herself," he says. "The girl who leased her before you was a bit too nervous to let her have a good gallop in the woods."

I don't think I've ever heard him say so much all at once. "Yeah. I'm enjoying it too. Where I lived before, there weren't a lot of trails."

"Where did you live before, anyway?"

"Ontario," I say.

His face brightens. "Me too. Whereabouts?"

My heart speeds up. Ontario is huge, I remind myself. Millions of people. "Georgetown," I say.

Tavish smacks his hand against his thigh. "No way."

I hold my breath. I feel like my heart has stopped beating.

"I used to live there," he says. "Well, just outside Georgetown, anyway."

I'm frantically calculating: He's older than me, and he's obviously lived out here for a while, and he definitely wasn't at Georgetown Middle School when I was there. He won't know Chloe or Patrice or anyone from my old school...but panic is rising inside me like a hot sticky wave, and my mind is racing ahead, ignoring my logic. What if he is still in touch with people from there? What if he mentions me? I picture him on the phone and imagine a guy's voice saying to him, *Sophie Keller? No way. She went to school with my little sister, I think. Complete loser, right?*

My heart is beating so hard and fast it feels like a woodpecker is trapped inside my rib cage. I swallow a wave of nausea and force myself to smile. "Small world," I say. Then I turn back to Keltie and slowly and methodically start cleaning the mud from her hooves.

Seventeen

IT'S ALMOST TEN o'clock that night when Zelia finally calls. Her voice is thick, as though she has been crying.

"Zelia?" I hesitate. "Are you okay?"

"No."

"Is it Josh? Did he break up with you?"

There is a pause.

"What are you talking about?" Zelia asks. She sounds irritated. "I'm not going out with Josh."

"You're not? But what about at the party? You and Josh?"

"Sophie, it was just sex. It doesn't mean we're a couple."

I can't help gasping. "You didn't."

"What? Oh. Not actually. People kept walking in, for one thing."

This is a dig at me, but I don't care. I'm just relieved she didn't have sex with Josh.

"Don't you think...I mean, shouldn't it be..."

Zelia interrupts. "Please. You sound like my mother. Wait till you're married, Zelia. Save it for someone special, Zelia. Men won't respect you if you are too easy, Zelia. God.

She's such a hypocrite. I'm so sick of it."

There is a long pause. I've never even kissed anyone, so I don't know what to say.

"So, what is wrong then?" I ask at last.

"It's Lee. She doesn't want me here."

"You live there. What do you mean she doesn't want you there?"

"She says she and Michael need some time alone. To *center* their relationship," Zelia says bitterly.

"Center?"

"I don't know. That's what she says."

"What does she want you to do then?"

"I could stay with you, if your mom says it's okay. Otherwise I have to go to my aunt's. But I don't want to. I'll miss school if I have to go there. I'm failing half my classes as it is."

"I can ask," I say. "I'll go ask. Hang on."

Mom is sitting at the kitchen table writing Christmas cards. She always does it early because she writes about a thousand of them. She still sends cards to parents of kids I went to preschool with. She never loses touch with anyone.

"Mom? Can Zelia come and stay?"

"Tonight?"

"No, I mean, for a while."

Mom frowns. "Why? For how long?"

I lean against the counter. "Lee says she has to come here or go to her aunt's."

"What?" Mom puts her pen down and brushes aside a lock of hair that has slipped out of her ponytail. "Did Zelia say why?"

"Not really." I make a face. "Oh, yeah. I guess Lee wants time alone with Michael."

Mom grimaces. "So she's kicking her daughter out?" She shakes her head quickly. "Sorry, I shouldn't have said that. It just makes me so…"

"So can she stay?"

"Are you sure you want her to?"

"Mom! She's my best friend."

My mother leans back, folds her hands together on top of the brightly colored cards littering the tabletop. She looks at me in silence for a moment. Then she says, "I wasn't sure if you two were getting along as well as you used to."

"Everything's fine," I say. "Besides, maybe if Zelia stays with us, things will be better. More like they used to be."

She studies my face. I can tell she wants to ask more about this, but she has always prided herself on not prying. Respecting my boundaries, she calls it.

"Let me think about it, okay?" she says at last.

"Mom! What am I supposed to tell her?"

She puts her pen down and pushes her chair back from the table. "Is she on the phone right now? Waiting?"

I nod.

Mom sighs. "Okay. Okay. She can come for a few days, but tell her I'll be calling Lee to make sure it's okay with her."

ZELIA ARRIVES LATE the next morning. I expected her to be subdued and unhappy, but she seems just the same as always.

"Michael dropped me off," she announces, dropping her duffel bag in the front hallway.

"Hi, Zelia." Mom pokes her head around the corner. "Everything okay?"

"Fine." Zelia gracefully balances on one foot as she pulls off her tall leather boots. "Thanks for letting me stay with you."

Mom smiles at her. "You're always welcome, Zelia. You know that."

"Come on," I say, picking up her duffel bag. Zelia follows me upstairs to my room.

"Your mom is so great," she says.

"She's okay."

Zelia unzips her duffel. "Look what Michael gave me," she says. She pulls a small blue jewelry box out of the bag and flips the lid open. Inside, a pair of small diamond earrings nestles against the dark velvet.

"Wow. Those are really pretty." I bend forward to look more closely but Zelia snaps the box shut.

"They're real," she says. "White gold with real diamonds."

"They're pretty," I say again. Even to my own ears, my voice sounds flat.

Zelia gives me a sharp look. "What's wrong? Are you pissed off about something?"

"No."

"Good. Because if anything, I'm the one that should be pissed off. Where did you take off to, anyways? At the party?"

I stare at her. "I left. You told me to, remember?"

Zelia blinks. "I didn't mean it, Sophie. I'm sorry. You know

I was just kidding, right?" She leans toward me and tilts her head to one side. "I looked everywhere for you, but you were gone."

"Max drove me home," I say.

"Max?" Zelia opens her eyes wide, like she doesn't know who Max is.

"You know Max."

"Well, yeah, sure. Black lipstick. One of the Goth triplets. Though I haven't actually seen her with her pals lately."

Zelia is looking at me expectantly. There is a long silence, which I refuse to fill. "So why did Max drive you home?" Zelia asks finally.

"Because I needed a ride, Zelia. Forget it. It's no big deal."

Zelia lifts her chin slightly and studies me from beneath her long lashes. "You seem different."

"I do?"

"Mmm." Zelia gives me a sudden conspiratorial grin. "It's going to be so great staying with you. I've missed our old talks, you know? We're going to have so much fun. Your mom is awesome for letting me come."

"I've missed our old talks too," I say softly.

Zelia lifts her hands and presses them against mine, fingertip to fingertip.

"Best friends forever," she whispers.

My heart leaps. "Best friends forever." It doesn't matter what Zelia does; she is still my beautiful crazy wonderful friend, and I still can't resist her.

Eighteen

AT LUNCH, MOM asks if I am still planning to ride. "I know you usually do on Sundays, but I thought, since Zelia is here…"

Max, Tavish and I had planned to ride together. I think again about yesterday's exhilarating ride. I remember Max's laughter and the light in Tavish's green eyes as they met mine. I'm not sure why, but I don't want Zelia to come to the barn. It feels like two worlds colliding. I wouldn't know how to act or who to be.

"I can skip it," I say quickly. "It doesn't matter."

"I don't want to mess up your family's plans, Dr. Keller." Zelia turns to me. "I could come too, couldn't I?"

And then I remember something else: Tavish used to live in Georgetown. My stomach tightens and clenches like a fist. I don't want to see him. And I definitely don't want Zelia to talk to him. "Maybe we should just hang out here," I say. "You'd probably be bored out at the barn."

Zelia picks up her fork and spears a piece of avocado from her salad. "I'd like to see where you ride," she says. "I won't be bored. I'd like to meet the horses. And your riding friends."

The kitchen is suddenly too hot, too small. I take a sip of cold water and feel it trace an icy path to my belly. Mom is watching me with that questioning look she gets—I think of it as her therapist expression.

I feel panicky, but I can't think of any way to get out of it without making Zelia wonder what's up. I don't want her to think I'm hiding something. I shrug, trying to look like it doesn't matter. "Okay then. We'll both go."

MOM DROPS US at the stables and blows me a kiss before she drives off. Sometimes I think she sees a lot more than I want her to.

As Zelia and I enter the barn, I can hear voices and laughter. Sebastian and Schooner are cross-tied in the aisle. Max is combing Sebastian's mane, and Tavish is sitting on a tack box lacing up his leather riding boots.

They look up as we enter. Max's face registers surprise and a flicker of some emotion I can't read; Tavish's face is open, friendly. The same as always, I think. Nothing has changed. He doesn't know anything about me. My stomach unknots itself, and I take a deep shaky breath.

"Hey, guys. Tavish, this is my friend Zelia." I look at Max. "She's staying with me for a few days."

Max nods. "Hi, Zelia."

I wish I could talk to Max. I want to explain, though I don't know what exactly I want to say or why I feel the need to explain anything.

"Are you riding with us?" Tavish asks.

"She doesn't ride," I say quickly.

Zelia strokes Sebastian's nose. "I've ridden a few times. At camp."

"She could ride Bug," Tavish says. "He's quiet. And he could use the exercise."

I shrug and turn to Zelia. "Do you want to come?" I half expect a rebuff, but to my surprise, Zelia's eyes are shining.

"I'd love to come," she says.

Max has been watching us, her face still and unreadable. Now she turns away and begins brushing out Sebastian's tail. I wonder what she is thinking.

I fetch Bug and Keltie. Tavish must have already groomed Bug today—the old gelding's coat has a soft gleam. Zelia seems relaxed and easy around the horses. She helps me groom Keltie, and we quickly tack up and follow the others outside.

Tavish finds a helmet that fits Zelia, and I give her a leg up into the saddle. She picks up the reins and sits straight-backed and relaxed. I lengthen the stirrup leathers for her; then I mount Keltie.

The trail is too narrow for all of us to ride side by side, so Tavish and Max ride ahead. They are laughing and chatting. I try to hear their conversation, but despite the clear windless weather, I can catch only fragments.

I look at Zelia, her black hair long and sleek beneath the black velvet riding hat, her hands relaxed on the reins. She looks like she has been riding all her life. Behind her, on the other side of the trail, the lake lies cold and still, its surface as smooth as glass.

She turns to me, blue eyes shining, lips curving in a contented smile, deep dimples in both cheeks. "This is wonderful," she says. Bug tosses his head and Zelia's clear laugh rings out.

"See?" she says. "He agrees with me."

"It is wonderful," I say softly. "I'm glad you came."

"Are you?" Zelia suddenly looks uncertain.

"Yes," I say, meaning it.

Zelia bends forward and strokes Bug's neck. Her hair falls forward, hiding her face. When she speaks, her voice is muffled.

"Sophie, I think I've really messed up."

"What do you mean?"

She turns toward me and her eyes are full of tears. I've never seen her cry before, and it scares me a little.

Zelia shakes her head. "I can't...I can't say anything. I can't tell." Her voice is wobbly. "Sophie, you're my friend, right? Best friends forever?"

"Best friends," I say. I mean to say the forever part too, but somehow I just don't.

She doesn't notice. "Okay. Because...Look, I'm not very good at apologizing, okay? But I know I've done some stupid things lately...All I'm trying to say is, you...I need you to keep being my friend, okay?"

I nod, feeling my own eyes fill with tears. "I will," I say helplessly. "Of course I will."

We ride in silence for a few minutes. I study the distorted reflections of the bare trees in the lake's smooth surface while Keltie's body moves smoothly beneath mine.

Max and Tavish have stopped their horses and are waiting

for us to catch up. When we reach them, Max twists in her saddle to face us, holding Sebastian's reins in one hand.

"How're you guys doing?" she asks. "Zelia, how do you like Bug?"

"He's all right," Zelia says offhandedly.

"You've ridden a bit before, right?" Max asks her.

"A few times."

"So are you up for a trot then?" Max looks at Zelia, and there is an unspoken challenge in her eyes. "I mean, we can just walk if you'd rather."

Zelia just shrugs. "Whatever."

I watch Zelia carefully. I know she can never resist a dare, and I feel responsible for her, out here in the woods.

Max nods and pushes Sebastian forward into a brisk trot. Tavish keeps Schooner alongside, and Zelia and I allow Bug and Keltie to match their pace. Zelia's hands are steady, her back straight. She posts neatly, rising and falling with the rhythm of Bug's gait.

I shake my head. "You can really ride. I can't believe you never told me."

Zelia's eyes are alive with laughter again. She is so different from me. When I am unhappy it takes forever for me to shake it off.

"I've only ridden a handful of times. Honestly."

"You're a natural then," I say, suppressing a small flash of jealousy as I recall my early riding lessons. It figures, somehow, that Zelia would instantly achieve a level of skill and ease that took me at least a year of hard work.

She grins at me, pleased. "Thanks."

Max turns and looks over her shoulder. "Okay back there?"

"Fine." I give her a thumbs-up.

"How about a canter? Is Zelia up for it?"

Zelia looks annoyed. "I have ears. You can talk to me, you know."

Max shrugs. "Sorry." She doesn't sound apologetic.

Zelia takes her reins in one hand and flips her hair back over her shoulder. "A canter is fine." She kicks Bug on and he leaps forward, looking a little indignant at her abruptness.

Tavish and Max quickly steady their horses as Bug barrels past them. Max scowls at me, and I shrug. I don't know what the hell is wrong with Max today or what is going on between her and Zelia.

I let Keltie ease forward into a canter and try to relax and enjoy the ride. A few horse-lengths ahead, Zelia is galloping, crouched like a jockey over Bug's back. She seems to be managing just fine.

Tavish brings Schooner up alongside me, and our two horses settle into an easy comfortable lope. He gives me a quizzical grin, one eyebrow raised. When he smiles, his whole face lights up and two lines crease his cheeks, framing his mouth like parentheses. I wonder how old he is. Older than me. Still in high school, though he doesn't go to our school. Seventeen, maybe.

I grin back.

Zelia has galloped out of sight around a bend in the trail, but we soon catch up to her. Bug is old, and while he's happy for a chance to run flat out, he won't go far at that speed.

He is trotting slowly, head low, breathing hard.

Zelia looks triumphant, exhilarated. "That was great," she says, looking directly at Max.

"You look pretty good on him," Max admits grudgingly.

Tavish laughs. "Pretty good? She looked like a pro."

For just a brief moment it feels okay, relaxed, like we could all be friends.

Zelia shrugs. "It's easy. Nothing to it. I don't know what the big deal is."

I glance up at Max, catch her rolling her eyes at Tavish and suddenly feel irritated with all three of them. A glance at my watch doesn't help; I didn't realize how late it was.

I swing Keltie around on the trail. "Zelia, we better get back to the barn," I say over my shoulder.

"I'll ride back with you," Tavish says.

Max gives me an apologetic half grin. "I should get back too." She turns Sebastian around and pulls up alongside me. "Let's go."

I look over at Zelia. She and Bug are standing a little way off, and her smile looks stiff on her face.

"Come on, Zelia," I say. "Mom's going to be waiting for us. And Bug's had enough for one day. He's an old guy. Let's get him home."

We ride back in silence, the air crackling with the tension of unspoken words.

Nineteen

MY MOM IS sitting in her car when we get back to the barn.

She honks the horn as soon as she sees us. "You're late!" she calls out the window. "Hurry up. I have a meeting at the university."

We quickly strip off saddles and bridles and turn Bug and Keltie out into the field. Zelia waves good-bye to Tavish, who gives her a quick grin but doesn't say anything. I look for Max, wanting to say good-bye, but she has disappeared.

"I'm sorry," I tell Mom. "I guess we lost track of time."

Mom just nods. She drives quickly home, rushes out to her office and flies past us again with her arms full of papers. "I'll be back around six," she says over her shoulder.

She's wearing lipstick, and I wonder if Patrick will be at the meeting.

Zelia helps herself to a can of Coke from the fridge. "That was so much fun," she says. She perches on a kitchen stool and takes a swig. "I don't know why I've never gone riding with you before."

"You usually have to have lessons and stuff," I say. "They don't just rent out the horses. You were lucky that Tavish let you ride Bug."

"Mmm. So what's the deal with him, anyway?"

I pick at my nail polish and try not to think about what Max said about Tavish liking me. I wish I didn't blush so easily. "Umm. What do you mean?"

"Like, does he work there or what?"

I look up. "Oh. That. Yeah, he mucks out stalls and exercises some of the horses. Bug's his horse. Tavish used to show him on the junior jumper circuit, but he retired him a couple of years ago. He shows other people's horses though…he's really good."

"Huh. He's kind of geeky though, don't you think?"

I shrug, feeling defensive. "I don't know. I've never noticed."

Zelia is quiet, and I wonder what she is thinking. I'm not sure why, but I don't want her thinking about Tavish.

"So, what do you want to do?" I ask.

Zelia shrugs. "Oh…I don't know. I need a smoke. Can we go outside for a minute?"

Since no one is home, we sit on the back steps. Zelia shakes two cigarettes out of her pack and hands one to me. I reach out automatically, but then I think of Max and I hesitate.

"Uh. No, thanks."

Zelia's eyes hold mine as she slides the cigarette back into the pack. She lights her own and takes a drag, still watching me.

"I hope you're not going to start giving me lectures about this," she says.

I shake my head. "You can do what you want," I say. "I just don't want one."

Zelia laughs skeptically. "Uh-huh."

I keep glancing at the neighbor's house. They have a clear view into our backyard, and I don't really want them to see Zelia smoking.

Finally, Zelia butts out her cigarette in her empty Coke can. "So. Let's go in your mom's office and hang out."

I hesitate. "Okay."

Mom's left the door unlocked, I guess because she was in such a rush. Zelia drops into one of the soft leather chairs and gestures for me to sit in the other.

She clears her throat. "So, Sophie," she says.

She is kidding around, talking in a phoney accent, but I feel anxious. I don't like this game, and I know Mom wouldn't want us coming in here without her permission.

"What brings you here today?" Zelia asks me.

"Well, Dr. Keenan," I begin, stalling while I think of something to say. "I have this problem…"

Zelia leans forward. "Tell me more about this… problem."

I stare at my hands. "Well…I keep chipping away at my nail polish. I have to reapply it at least once a day."

Zelia frowns. "But, Sophie, this is serious. This is a serious problem. Tell me why you do this."

Through the window I can see the bare branches of the weeping willow waving in the wind, skinny arms twisting against the gray sky.

"I don't know," I say. "I guess it gives me something to do with my hands."

"Aha," says Zelia. "I see."

"Aha?"

"Aha. I understand. It is obvious you are afraid of sex."

I snort. "That's ridiculous. Just because I—"

Zelia frowns. "Do not call Dr. Keenan ridiculous. Dr. Keenan is a highly respected headshrinker."

I giggle. "Mom hates that expression."

"No doubt." Zelia leans back and puts her feet up on the coffee table. "Okay. My turn."

I hesitate. I know Zelia has set this up deliberately, but I want to ask her what is wrong for real. It doesn't seem right to make it a game.

"Go on," she says. "Ask me."

Zelia's eyes are too bright, her face too flushed. She looks feverish.

"Ask me," she insists. The words are as tight and hard as two fists.

So I do. I lean forward and say, "So, Zelia. Tell me why you are here. Tell me...tell me what is wrong."

Zelia is quiet for a moment. She takes her feet off the coffee table and tucks them underneath her in the black leather armchair.

"Dr. Keller," she says.

She isn't looking at me. Her eyes are fixed on the tall shelves lined with my mother's books: *The Therapist's Use of Self; Transference and Counter-Transference; Trauma and Recovery.*

I wonder if she wishes she was talking to my mother instead of me.

"Yes," I say. Then I just wait. My heart is beating hard: tell me, tell me, tell me.

Zelia closes her eyes for a moment; then she opens them and looks at me. "I think I'm in love," she says.

"With Josh?" I ask.

She looks at me blankly for a moment, and then she shakes her head. "No. No. With Michael."

"Michael?" For a moment I can't think who she means. Then, heart sinking, I realize who she must be talking about.

"Not—not your mom's boyfriend? That Michael?"

Zelia frowns at me. "Dr. Keller," she reproaches, shaking her index finger at me. "Aren't you supposed to be calm and nonjudgmental?"

"Right. Right." I collect myself, rearrange my features. My head is spinning. "So. You say you are in love with your mother's boyfriend, Michael. Is he aware of your feelings?"

Zelia nods.

"So…" I can't think clearly, so I fall back on Zelia's line. "Tell me more about this."

Zelia leans toward me. "This is all confidential, right?"

I nod. "Don't worry. I won't tell anyone."

"Okay." She tugs at the frayed ends of her over-long sleeves and tucks her hands inside. "Okay."

I wait silently. It is starting to get dark outside. The sun sets so early now. I wish I had turned on a light, but I don't want to interrupt her story, so I just sit and watch her face in the darkening room.

"I liked him," she says suddenly. "I know I said I hated him, but I didn't really. He was nice to me. He listened. I told him some stuff, about not knowing my dad, you know?"

"Yeah."

"He really listened." She meets my eyes briefly. "Lee never listens."

I nod.

"We'd sit and talk for hours," she says softly. "About everything, you know? About life."

I think I know where this story is going. I don't want to hear it. Part of me wants to put my hands over my ears like a little kid: *La la la, I can't hear you.* But another part of me is fascinated.

"I could tell he was attracted to me," Zelia says.

Her voice is hushed. Behind her, the wall clock is ticking too loudly.

"I would see him looking at me. Always looking at me."

"That's...that's not right," I blurt out.

Zelia frowns. "Dr. Keller, I'd appreciate it if you could keep your judgments to yourself."

I don't want to play this game anymore. I wish it really was my mother sitting here listening to Zelia's story. She'd know what to say.

"Anyway," Zelia continues, "he moved in and we were having these intense conversations all the time...and then he and Lee would be doing their lovey-dovey thing. All over each other. And I hated it. I hated it."

"I remember that," I say. I am trying to fit this new version with what I thought I knew, going back over our conversations. "So…then what happened?"

Zelia's eyes meet mine and hold on tight. Her pupils are huge inky pools in her pale face.

"One night Lee was out, and Michael and I were talking. On the couch. I could see him, see how he was looking at me. I just felt like I could do anything, you know?"

"Uh-huh." I don't know, not really.

"And I just…I just put my hand on his leg, you know? That's all. But he let me. He didn't say anything. We just kept on talking."

Her gaze doesn't waver, but I turn away and look outside at the darkening sky and the bare branches of the willow.

"Maybe I should turn on a light," I say.

"Just—just listen, Sophie."

There is a note in her voice that I have rarely heard. A plea, almost. And she has called me Sophie, not Dr. Keller. I meet her eyes. "Okay."

Zelia leans across the table and puts her hand on my arm. "It was crazy. The next day, my mom sent me off to my aunt's place. I swear, it was like she knew. She was jealous."

"Do you think he told her?"

Zelia gives a short scornful laugh and lets go of my arm. "As if. He's not crazy."

"So…"

"So, I don't know. Maybe she saw how he looked at me.

Maybe she could tell he was falling for me. Anyway, when I came back, he acted all distant. Like nothing had happened. I couldn't believe it. So as soon as I had a chance, I pulled him into my room and told him I had to talk to him."

"And? What did you say?" I hold my breath.

"Nothing." She smiles and winks at me. "I just started kissing him."

"Oh my god. You didn't."

"I did. And he kissed me back." Zelia leans back and half closes her eyes. "Sophie, it was so hot."

"Zelia! He's like…old. And he's Lee's boyfriend."

She laughs. "Well, he sure kisses better than guys our age." Her eyebrows draw together, and she stops laughing. "Then all of a sudden he just pushed me away. Just pushed me away and said I was crazy. And walked out the door."

"And…"

"And that was the day after the party. Right before I called you and asked if I could come here."

"You said Lee kicked you out…"

"I know. Well, she did. But I wanted to go. I couldn't stand being there."

I let out a long sigh. "So, I guess that's it? It's over—you and Michael?"

Zelia shakes her head and her lips curve in a cat-like smile. "I don't think so. Because, just before I left, he slipped those earrings into my hand."

A beam of light pierces the darkness, suddenly illuminating the room. I turn quickly to the window.

"Mom's home," I say. "Come on. We shouldn't be out here."

Zelia uncurls her legs and follows me. We duck in the back door just as my mother pulls the front door shut behind her.

Twenty

THE NEXT WEEK, Zelia and I walk to school together every day. We don't talk about Michael. She doesn't bring it up again, and I'm relieved. We don't talk about our own lives at all. Walking to and from school, we play our old games—watching people and making up stories about them. We spend lunch hours in the smoking area, often just the two of us, though sometimes we hang out with Jas and Maisie.

"How come Max never hangs out with you guys anymore?" I ask them one day.

They exchange a meaningful glance, and then Jas turns to me and shrugs. "She's doing her own thing these days," she says. "Doesn't really have time for us."

I feel like there's something she's not saying.

Maisie just nods. "She's a bit of a loner. Max kind of comes and goes when she wants, you know? Anyway, she finds it hard to be around smokers since she quit."

A couple of times, Zelia and I go out to the barn together after school. Max isn't there and neither, to my relief, is Tavish. Zelia sits on the fence and watches me practice leg yielding and half passes in the cold drizzling rain.

The air is heavy and damp, and everything feels slow and tired. I feel like I am waiting for something to happen.

That weekend, it does. My mother has gone out to her yoga class, and Zelia and I are sitting at the dining room table, working on a paper for Mr. Farley's English class. It's about *Lord of the Flies*. I read the book in one night and then lay awake for hours, my stomach twisted so tight I could hardly breathe. I didn't know boys were like that too. I thought it was just girls who had the kind of radar that detected weakness, just girls who were vicious to each other when no adults were around. Mr. Farley suggested we talk about one theme, but all I can think about is my middle school back in Georgetown.

Zelia puts her pen down and flips her notebook shut. "I'm going outside for a smoke."

I just nod and keep staring at my blank page.

HALF AN HOUR later, I still haven't written anything, and Zelia hasn't come back. I get up, stretch and wander outside to find her.

The door to Mom's office is open. I walk down the path and peer inside. Zelia is sitting on the floor, legs crossed, a pile of papers on her lap.

"What are you doing?" I ask, bewildered.

Beside her is my mother's tall gray filing cabinet. The top drawer is open, and files are scattered on the carpet.

"Zelia! Oh my god. What are you doing?" I grab files and start shoving them back in the drawer.

Zelia looks up. "Take it easy, Sophie."

"These are my mom's client files! They're supposed to be totally confidential. She always keeps them locked up."

"Yeah, well, the key was in her desk drawer." Zelia closes the file she was looking at. "You should check this one out, Sophie. She's a real winner. A Tiffany, I bet. She's been having an affair and now she's—"

I grab the file. "Shut up, Zelia. Just shut up. I don't want to know." I'm almost crying now. I can't help it. I cram the file back in the drawer. I know they'll all be out of order, but I just want to get Zelia out of here.

"Why?" I ask. "Why would you do this?" My voice comes out in a wail. I feel sick.

Zelia stands up. "Jeez, Sophie. Relax. I just wondered if your mom had ever seen Michael, you know, as a client. But I guess not, I couldn't find a file for him. And then I just was wondering what kind of—"

She breaks off, eyes suddenly wide and fixed over my shoulder.

"What?" I turn around slowly.

Behind me, framed in the open door, stands my mother. Her long hair is pulled back in a loose ponytail, and she is wearing a snug T-shirt and black yoga pants. She looks like she has just been slapped. I can actually see the color drain from her face and then flood back in an angry rush of heat.

"Mom," I begin.

"What exactly is going on here?" she asks slowly. Her gaze takes in the open filing cabinet, the loose pages still on the floor. She shakes her head and her voice comes out loud and cracked. "What the hell do you two think you are doing?" She rushes forward and begins gathering up the papers.

"Mom," I say tentatively.

She straightens, clutching the loose pages to her chest, and I notice with a sickening sense of shock that she actually has tears in her eyes.

"How could you let this happen, Sophie? How could you?" Her voice is shaking. "People come here and tell me the most private things…My god, Sophie. You know enough about my work to know what you've done. To know how much of a betrayal this is."

I start to cry. "Mom, I didn't…I mean, I wasn't even…"

We stare at each other for a moment. The room is silent except for the ugly choking sound of my sobs. Beside me, Zelia is motionless.

My mom takes a deep breath. "Sophie, I'm only going to ask you this once, and I want the truth. Did you have anything to do with this? Anything at all?"

I dig my nails into my hands and swallow my tears. I shake my head.

"I want an answer, Sophie."

"No," I whisper, "I didn't."

"Zelia, I think you'd better pack your things and go home," my mother says. Her eyes don't waver from my face.

"But, Dr. Keller—"

"Now." My mother's voice is as sharp and cold as ice.

Zelia stares at my mother, wide-eyed. She opens her mouth slightly, as if she is about to argue; then she turns and runs from the room.

As soon as she is gone, I start crying again. "I'm sorry, I'm so sorry. I was working on my paper…I didn't know…"

"Sophie, do you have any idea, any idea at all, how serious this is?"

I don't think I have ever seen my mother so angry.

"I know." I choke the words out past the hard aching lump in my throat. "I'm so sorry."

Mom is staring at the files sticking haphazardly out of the gaping drawer. "I'm absolutely disgusted," she says. "I am just so disappointed in you. How can I trust you after this?"

"I'm sorry," I say again. I don't know what else I can say.

"Go on," she says. "You better go say good-bye to Zelia. I'm going to clean up this…this mess…and I want her out of the house by the time I'm done."

I hesitate. "Mom…I don't know if Lee will let her go home."

Mom raises her voice. "Sophie, do not, *do not*, try to make this my problem. Lee will just have to deal with it."

I back away from her slowly, wanting to say something more. To explain. But I don't even know where to begin. There are so many things I haven't told her, starting with everything that happened back in Georgetown. When I decided to leave the old Sophie behind, somehow I left my mother behind too.

I turn away and run into the house.

In my bedroom, Zelia is throwing her clothes into her duffel bag.

She looks up as I come in. "Thanks a lot, Sophie," she says bitterly. "Just let me take all the blame."

I can't believe I heard her correctly. "What? I didn't have anything to do with it. Do you have any idea how much trouble you got me into?"

Zelia crams the last of her things into the bag and yanks the zipper closed. It jams, and she swears and kicks the bag in frustration.

"I can't fucking *deal* with this," she yells. "What the hell am I supposed to do now?"

I slump on the edge of the bed. "You better call Lee. See if she can come pick you up."

Zelia jerks the zipper free and closes it. "Fine. Fine."

She picks up the phone and turns to me, raises one eyebrow. "God. Talk about overreacting though." She gives a half grin. "Did you see your mom's face?"

I can't meet her eyes. "You better just go," I say.

"Lighten up, Sophie. It was just a bunch of stuff about some losers who like to talk about their problems."

Something snaps inside me and comes loose. "Shut up," I say, standing up. "Shut up."

Zelia looks startled. "Sophie…"

Anger is rising inside me like a hot suffocating wave. I dig my fingernails into my palms, but I can't stop the words from spilling out. "Did you ever think that maybe *you* should be talking to someone about your problems, Zelia? That maybe it isn't all that normal to only be able to talk to your best friend when you're pretending she's a shrink? That maybe fooling around with your mom's boyfriend is just messed up?"

Zelia takes a step toward me and grabs my wrist, hard. "And you've got it all together?" she hisses.

I hold my breath. Her eyes are a hot pale blue; they burn holes in me. I can't look away.

"Don't bother calling me," she says. She throws my arm back at me, grabs her bag and is gone.

I stare after her for a moment. Her boots pound down the stairs, and the front door slams shut behind her with a hollow bang. I can still feel her cold fingers on my wrist, like icy handcuffs. I drop onto my bed, bury my face in my pillow and cry.

Twenty-one

I MUST HAVE fallen asleep, because it is dark when Mom comes up to my room. She sits on the edge of my bed and puts her hand on my forehead, like she is checking to see if I have a fever.

"Mom," I say. "I didn't—"

"I know," she says.

We are both quiet for a moment. She sighs and takes her hand off my head. I want to grab her hand and hold it tight, put it back on my head and keep it there, but of course I don't.

"She can't stay here anymore," Mom says.

I roll over and look at her. Part of me wants to argue, but there's nothing I can say. I swallow hard. "I know. I'm sorry, Mom. I really am."

She looks so sad. "Me too."

I think of all the times Zelia has followed my mom around, talking to her, asking her questions. I remember how I used to think that perhaps Zelia just hung out with me because she liked my mother. "You like Zelia, though. Right? You've always liked her."

Mom pulls the elastic off her ponytail and shakes her hair loose. She switches on the light on my bedside table and sighs. "I feel bad for her. I don't think she's had an easy life."

"You do like her, though?" I ask stubbornly.

Mom hesitates. "It's not that I don't like her…really, it isn't. I just think she hasn't always been very nice to you. I think… I don't always trust her. I think Zelia cares most of all about Zelia."

I am quiet for a moment. "I'm so sorry about what happened. I couldn't believe it when I saw…"

Mom stands up. "I know, Sophie. I know."

THAT EVENING I call Max. "Are you riding tomorrow?"

Max's voice is guarded. "I'm planning to."

I hesitate. "I didn't see you at school last week," I say. Something about Max always makes me wary of asking too many questions. She seems so straightforward, but there's something very private about her. Like she'll let people in so far, and then that's it. "Jas and Maisie said you were doing your own thing…"

"Yeah. I've been going to the library at lunch. I screwed around last year, so I need to pull my grades up. Anyway, the smoking thing, you know…"

"I quit too," I offer.

"You did?"

I want Max to be pleased. "Yeah. I did."

"Good."

"So." I feel shy and awkward. "So, I guess I'll see you at the barn then. Tomorrow morning?"

"I'll be out there around nine."

There is a pause, and then Max asks, "Is Zelia coming too?"

"No. No, just me."

"Okay then," Max says. "I'll see you there."

I hang up and sit there for a minute, grinning foolishly at the telephone.

THE NEXT DAY is bright, clear and cold. Out at the barn, the horses are all impatient and eager to get outside. Keltie dances around, swinging her head up and down as I mount.

Max is trotting Sebastian in circles in the ring, trying to get him settled down before we go into the woods. Keltie can be silly sometimes, and she likes to go fast, but Sebastian is a bit of a nut. At four, he's still a youngster, but he's almost seventeen hands high—huge and very strong. He spooks all the time, taking great leaps sideways and running away from things only he can see.

I wave to Max, and she turns Sebastian toward us, trotting slowly onto the trail that leads to the woods. I haven't seen her since the time I was here with Zelia. It was just last weekend, but it feels so long ago.

"Hey." Max slows to a walk so that I can bring Keltie alongside.

"Hey." I grin up at her. "It's good to see you."

"You too," she says, grinning back at me. "I've missed you this week. Had to look after the twins a lot after school. Mom's aunt died and she had to go to the mainland for the funeral." She slaps Sebastian's neck affectionately. "Missed riding too. This big lunatic is wild today—he hasn't been out all week."

We ride in silence for a while. There was a frost last night, and a thin crust of frozen mud crunches beneath the horses' hooves. The sun shines small and white against the blue sky. I breathe deeply. The outlines of the bare branches look sharp and distinct in the morning light.

Keltie is excited by the cold clear weather. Her steps are springy and she keeps snorting and throwing her head up joyfully.

Alongside, Max is struggling to keep Sebastian calm. He is dancing along, the whites of his eyes showing and his nostrils flared. She nods an apology to me and lets the big Thoroughbred pull ahead. I drop into single file behind her and watch her sitting deep and relaxed in the saddle. She is good, really good. I wouldn't want to be riding Sebastian today.

"Hey, Max," I call out.

"Yeah."

"Okay up there?"

She laughs. "He's a head case, but I'm used to him. We're fine."

We ride on in silence for a few minutes. Usually I enjoy this, but today I want to talk to her. I watch, frowning a little. Her legs are glued to her horse's sides, and I know that it is taking all her strength and concentration to keep Sebastian's wild energy in check.

"Are you busy later? Do you want to come over?" I shout.

Max glances over her shoulder at me. "Isn't Zelia staying with you? Because I don't want to be, you know..."

"No," I tell her, "she left."

BACK AT THE barn, I borrow Max's phone and call my mom to tell her that Max will drive me home. We are about to get in Max's car when Tavish pulls up in a pickup truck piled with horse feed and other supplies. He leans out the window and calls over to us.

"Hey, Max, Sophie. Are you guys riding?"

"We did already. We're just leaving." Max unlocks the passenger-side door and opens it for me.

"Too bad," Tavish says, getting out of the truck. He looks disappointed. "I've been running all kinds of errands this week. Haven't had time to ride as much as I should."

I'm standing with one foot in the car. "Maybe this week? I'll be coming out most days after school."

He brightens and pushes his floppy brown hair out of his eyes. "That'd be great. Really great."

When Tavish grins, his green eyes narrow into little triangles, and laugh lines stretch toward his temples and down his cheeks. You can tell where his wrinkles will be when he's old. Even though it's almost December, his face is still tanned from working outside so much. His teeth are slightly crooked and very white.

I wish he was from anywhere but Georgetown.

"Come on," Max says, getting into the car. "See you, Tavish."

I realize I am staring and quickly slip the rest of the way into the car.

Max starts the engine and backs up. Tavish waves; then he turns and begins unloading the truck.

"I don't know how he does it," she says.

"Does what?"

"Oh, he just works a lot of hours here. You know? And he's in grade twelve, so he has a lot of schoolwork too. Though I don't think school is really his thing. He really wants to ride professionally, and it's hard if you don't have money."

This is all new to me. It is a bit of a shock to realize I don't know much about Tavish. We've only ever talked about horses. I didn't realize Max knew him so well.

"How long has he lived here?" I blurt.

She looks surprised. "Ages. Since he was a kid, I think. Why?"

I breathe a sigh of relief. "Just wondered. So…do you like him?" I ask.

"He's a great guy," she says. "A smart, honest, no-bullshit guy."

I shake my head, watching her serious face. "No, I mean… do you *like* him?"

Max takes her eyes off the road for a minute and looks at me. She laughs. "No," she says, "not me."

We drive by a field that was full of pumpkins a few weeks ago. Now, with Halloween long over, it is brown and bare.

Max tilts her head to one side. "Do you?" she asks.

I shake my head in confusion. I know I am blushing. "I don't know," I say.

Max drums her fingers against the steering wheel. Her expression is hard to read. "He's a stellar guy," she says.

We are almost back at my place when Max asks abruptly, "So Zelia went home?"

I sigh. "We kind of had a fight."

Max opens her mouth and shuts it again.

"What?" I say.

"Nothing."

"No, go on. What were you going to say?"

Max pulls a pack of gum out of her pocket and offers it to me. I shake my head. She pops a piece out of the bubble pack and sticks it in her mouth. "You and Zelia. It's none of my business."

I twist in my seat so that I am facing her. "It's okay," I say. "I know you don't like her."

Max frowns, dark eyebrows drawing together. In the bright sunlight pouring through the windshield, I can see a scattering of pale golden freckles across her nose and upper cheeks.

"I don't exactly dislike her either," she says judiciously. "I just don't really get what you see in her."

I'm quiet for a moment, thinking. How can I explain Zelia's magnetism, the irresistible energy that pulls me into her orbit and holds me there? Even though she can make me crazy— even though she does awful things sometimes—I can't imagine my life without her in it.

"I didn't know anyone when we moved here," I say. "Zelia just kind of…drew me in. I don't know how to describe it." I stare out the window and squint into the sun. "She's different," I say. "She's kind of exciting, I guess."

Max says nothing. Images of Zelia are flickering through my mind: Zelia drawing dark eyeliner along the inner edges of her eyes; Zelia sitting beside me on the sidewalk while my grandmother stares at the hat by our feet; Zelia lying on her bed, a blue stone twinkling in her freshly pierced navel; Zelia pulling down her sleeve to cover the cut on her arm; Zelia sitting on the floor in my mom's office, open files scattered around her.

"I'm worried about her," I say softly.

We pull up in front of my house. Max parks the car and turns to look at me.

"Worried about her? How come?"

I want to tell Max about Michael, but I promised I wouldn't tell anyone. "She does things, sometimes…that aren't good. Aren't good for her, I mean."

Max looks serious. "Like what?"

Michael, I think. Shoplifting. So many things.

"I promised I wouldn't tell anyone," I say. "But then we had this fight, and she left, and…I don't know. I hope she's okay, that's all."

Max is quiet for a moment. "What did you fight about?" she asks. "I mean, if you want to talk about it."

I look straight ahead. Down the driveway, I can see the door to my mother's office. I feel sick to my stomach every time I think about the reason we fought. "I don't think I really want to talk about it," I say. I scrape mud off the heel of one boot with the toe of the other. "She did something really stupid. Something she shouldn't have done."

Max sighs and opens her door. "I don't want to sound too harsh, but that's her problem. Not yours."

I open my door and realize I've got mud all over the floor of Max's car. "I guess."

We get out of the car and stand in the driveway for a moment in silence; then Max says, "You know that thing you told me? About the sculptor and the figures in the stone?"

I nod.

"Well, maybe Zelia's just chipping away at the marble, you know?"

"Maybe," I say. I know Max is trying to help, but a feeling of foreboding is lying heavy in my belly and tightening like a band around my forehead.

Mom's in the kitchen making baklava, placing layer after layer of fragile phyllo pastry into a shallow glass tray. Back when I still ate dessert, baklava was my favorite. I figure that's why she's making it—she's always trying to persuade me to eat.

She looks up and smiles at us. "You must be Max," she says, wiping her hands on a dishtowel.

Max shakes her hand. "Nice to meet you."

I can tell Mom is studying Max carefully, probably trying to figure out whether she's going to be a good influence or not. It suddenly feels important to me that my mother like her.

"Max has twin brothers," I offer inanely. "She babysits them a lot."

Both Max and my mother turn and look at me blankly.

"That's great," Mom says.

I silently vow to keep my mouth shut.

"I have to go out in a bit to pick up things for dinner," she says. "Sophie, I don't want you two going in my office, okay?"

I blush furiously. She knows it wasn't my fault. She didn't have to say that.

"We won't," I say.

Mom looks me in the eyes. "Okay." She turns to Max. "Are you staying for dinner?"

"Oh no, that's okay," Max says quickly.

"It's no trouble. I'm just going to pick up a frozen pizza or something."

"Stay," I urge her. "Stay for dinner."

Max shakes her head and looks at my mother. "It's really nice of you but I have to go home in a bit." She starts to laugh. "I'm babysitting the twins tonight."

UP IN MY room, Max seems uneasy. She sits on the beanbag chair; then she gets up and looks out the window.

"Clouding over," she says.

I flop onto my bed and stretch out. "Mmm-hmm. You okay, Max?"

Max nods. She sits down cross-legged beside me. "Sophie... there's something I really want to tell you." She hesitates before going on. "I've been wanting to tell you this for ages, but I don't know how you'll react and I—well, you're important to me, you know?" Max's dark eyes are fixed on the bedspread, her face turned downward.

"What is it?" I say. "You can tell me."

"Okay."

There is a long silence. "Well, remember when I…you know, the night of the party…"

"Uh-huh."

There is another long silence. Finally Max shakes her head. "You know, this isn't a good idea. Forget it. It's nothing."

I prop myself up on my elbows and tilt my head to one side, trying to read her expression. "It's okay, Max. Tell me."

"I shouldn't have brought it up."

I sit up and lean toward her. "Max! You're making me crazy! What is it?" I think about what she said in her car that time, about how you can't always be honest about yourself.

Max shakes her head and her eyes are wet. She blinks furiously. "Damn it. Can we change the subject?"

I wish she would tell me. I remember that night at Max's place, how I whispered my secrets into the dark when I knew she was sleeping.

"Max," I say hesitantly.

"What?"

"There's something I want to tell you too."

"There is?" Max brushes the back of her hand roughly across her eyes. "Tell me then."

"You know how I used to live in Ontario? In Georgetown?" Max nods.

"Well…don't tell anyone this, okay?"

"I won't."

I want Max to know me. I want to tell her the truth, but it's hard. Having kept it a secret for so long makes it seem like such a big deal. "I should have told you this before," I say. "When we first started getting to know each other. I don't know. I feel like I'm doing everything backward, telling you now. All out of order."

"It's okay," Max says. "Just tell me. If you want to."

I sigh. "I was…different then, you know? In middle school. Grade eight and nine."

"Yeah? Well, I guess we all were."

I pick at a loose thread on the quilt. "No, I mean, I was really…I got picked on a lot. Bullied, I guess you'd call it."

Max looks surprised, but her voice is soft. "Sophie, I'm really sorry. That's awful."

"It was my fault, really. I was such a loser."

Max frowns. "No one deserves to be bullied."

"No, I know." I want to make sure she understands. "All I'm saying is that I wasn't like I am now. I didn't fit in, you know? I was kind of fat. I wore stupid clothes. I acted like a little kid. Stuff like that."

Max interrupts me. "That's a load of crap. You're just letting the kids who bullied you off the hook. How come you're not mad at them?" Her voice is getting loud.

I'm not sure what reaction I had expected, but this wasn't it. I think for a moment. "I don't know. I guess maybe I should be?"

"Damn right you should," Max says passionately. "No one

has a right to treat you like that. No one should make you feel bad about yourself."

Something inside me loosens, lightens. I meet Max's eyes. Relief is bubbling up from deep inside me. She knows and she doesn't care. More than that: She knows and she's on my side.

I reach out and touch her hand. "Thanks," I say softly.

Max shrugs. "Just saying what I think."

I laugh. "Yeah, I know. You do that." That's why I trust her, I think. She never says anything she doesn't mean.

It's only later that I realize she never told me her own secret.

Twenty-two

I SPEND THE evening working on my English paper. I've written pages and pages, but I won't be able to hand it in. It's by far the weirdest paper I've ever written. It has bits of poems tossed in, and sketches of scared faces and echoes of voices from my own past. It's about *Lord of the Flies*, I guess, but it's about Georgetown and Chloe and Patrice too.

It's a paper about things falling apart, and if I hand it in, Mr. Farley will be calling my mother for sure. I sigh and try to figure out if I can salvage anything useful from the mess of words. I've never had a grade below an A– in my life. I wouldn't admit this to anyone—I took enough crap about being a keener back in Georgetown—but I don't really want to start screwing my grades up now.

Every couple of minutes I glance at the phone. I try not to think about Zelia. If she doesn't call, then forget it—I'm not calling her. She's the one who owes me an apology. I look at the phone again. Zelia never apologizes. If she calls, she'll be full of bright chatter, reeling me back in like a fish with a hook through its lip. She'll pretend nothing happened.

THE NEXT DAY, Zelia doesn't show up for school. At lunchtime I wait by Max's locker and persuade her to go for a walk with me. It's still clear and sunny outside, and we walk through the little square, browse in the small gallery on the corner, sit and talk on the steps in front of the theater.

"Did you bring lunch?" Max asks.

I shake my head.

"Come on, I'll buy you something." Max pulls me into the pizza place and orders a slice for herself. "What do you want?"

"Coffee?"

"You have to eat something. Come on, Sophie. I'm buying."

Max is watching me intently.

I scan the menu. "Umm, okay. Vegetarian pizza then. Thanks."

We sit at a small round table in the back corner. After the bright sunlight, the café is dark and quiet.

"Have you heard from Zelia yet?" Max asks.

"No, and she's not at school today."

Max gives me a look. "Yeah, well, I figured you wouldn't be hanging out with me if she was."

I lean across the table. "I'm sorry. It's not that I'd rather be with her, you know. Honestly. I wish…I don't know…it's just that I was friends with her first."

Max takes a bite of pizza. She chews slowly and swallows before answering. "I know. It's okay. I didn't say that to make you feel bad. My feelings aren't hurt or anything. It's just a fact."

I shake my head. "Max…"

She shushes me. "It's okay. I just…you're pretty easy to talk to, you know? I like hanging out with you. But I don't want to cause problems for you. Or Zelia."

I stare at my pizza. "Max?"

"Yeah."

"Zelia…she was shoplifting. And I think she might have cut herself, one time. On purpose."

Max puts her elbows on the table and balances her chin on her folded hands. "I guess that's what you meant when you said she was doing things that weren't good for her."

I pick a mushroom off my pizza and chew it slowly. "Other stuff too. I'm…I'm worried about her."

Max is watching me silently.

"What?" I say.

Frowning, she unfolds her hands, pulls the straw out of her glass of water and sticks one end in her mouth.

"What?" I ask again.

"Promise you won't get mad."

"It's okay," I say. "I know you don't like Zelia much."

Max holds the straw like it's a cigarette, between two fingers. "It's not about Zelia exactly."

I stare at her. "Tell me, already."

She points at my cold congealing pizza with her straw. "You. Never eating. Thinking you're fat. How is that any different from what Zelia is doing?"

I stare at her. I want to argue, to tell her it's not the same, but her eyes hold mine, dark and steady, and the words dissolve like salt in my mouth.

Max gives a little shrug and sticks her straw back in her glass. "Just think about it, okay?"

There is a roaring in my ears and a lump in my throat, and I'm scared I might start to cry. I nod. "Okay," I whisper.

THAT NIGHT, I undress in front of the bathroom mirror. I look at myself, trying to be objective. My ribs are sharply outlined, my chest bony, my shoulders knobby, my arms and legs long and angular. *See*, I tell an imaginary Max, *I know I'm skinny. I can see I'm too skinny. I'm not crazy. I just don't want to get fat, that's all.*

Mom knocks on the door. "Sophie? Are you almost done in there? I wouldn't mind taking a quick bath before I go to bed."

I pull an oversize T-shirt over my head, brush my teeth and retreat to my bedroom. I drop to my knees and jerk open the stiff bottom drawer of my dresser. All the stuff Zelia gave me—the stuff she stole—is crammed in here. I scoop it out—makeup, jewelry, sunglasses—and wonder if I should get rid of it.

Underneath it all lies a red photo album. I run my hand over the cheap plastic cover and try to remember when I last looked at these pictures. Not since we left Georgetown. A lifetime ago.

I flip open the front cover. There I am with Dragonfly, the tall gray mare I used to ride. I turn the pages, slowly at first and then faster. Staring. I'm not seeing what I expected to see. These pictures don't fit with my memories.

I stop and scrutinize my grade nine self. I am standing on a bale of hay, reaching up to braid Dragonfly's forelock. My hair is longer and lighter, and my body looks different—stronger, more solid—but I look fine. I am smiling into the camera and I'm not fat. I'm not fat at all. I trace the tiny outline of my face with my fingertip, confused.

My mom took this picture. I can remember it clearly. It was early one spring morning, not long before we moved, and I was getting ready for a schooling show. We got to the barn at 6:00 AM and my mother, who doesn't even like horses, helped me wash Dragonfly, braid her mane and groom her to perfection. It was my first show, and Dragonfly and I placed first in an equitation class and second over fences. It was a good day—a great day.

I look at the picture again, trying to clear the fog in my head. The old Sophie looks a little different, I guess. Younger. And I definitely have a better haircut now. But there is nothing in this photograph to explain the things that happened, nothing to explain the shoves in the hall, the names I was called. Nothing to explain two years of no friends. Nothing to explain my believing that I was fat.

There is a knock at the door. I quickly shove all Zelia's stolen stuff back into the drawer and drop the photo album on top. "Come in."

Mom opens the door a few inches and pokes her head in.

"Hi, Sophie," she says. "I'm just off to bed."

"Okay. 'Night."

She stands there for a moment, looking at me. "Sophie…"

"What?"

She opens her mouth. Then she shuts it again and smiles tentatively. "Nothing. Just good night, that's all."

I think about that photograph, about her helping me with Dragonfly that morning. I wish Mom would come into my room, sit on my bed and talk to me like she used to talk to the old Sophie Keller. I want to ask her why those girls used to call me fat and why I believed them. I want to know why they wrote those words on my locker. I want everything to feel okay between us again.

I look at her, standing there in her nightdress, a towel tied around her wet hair. I don't know why I never told her about the bullying. I just never told anyone.

"Good night," I say.

I AM ASLEEP when the phone rings twice and stops. The digital alarm clock beside my bed says 11:52. I wonder who would call this late. My first thought is of Gran: Is she okay? What if she has had a heart attack or something? I slip out of bed and tiptoe down the hall toward my mother's bedroom. Her door is open a crack and the soft light of her reading lamp spills out into the dark hallway. I stand close and strain to hear what she is saying.

"Is she okay?"

It is Gran, I think. I push my hands against my chest. My heart is fluttering oddly. For the first time, I really grasp that Gran is Mom's mother, just like Mom is my own, and even though I don't like Gran very much, I want desperately for her to be okay.

"So they're keeping her in the hospital?" my mother asks. Her voice is surprisingly calm. All I can think is that I've never really talked to Gran. We haven't even gotten to know each other. She never did tell my mother about that day she caught Zelia and me panhandling, and again I wonder why not.

"Okay," my mother says. A pause. "Okay, I will." Another long pause.

I feel frantic with anxiety. I dig my bare toes into the carpet and wonder whether I should go in.

"Not tonight," she is saying. "It's almost midnight. I'm not waking her up."

I slip through the door. "Mom," I whisper. "It's okay, I'm up."

Mom is sitting up in bed, covers pulled over her bent knees. She looks up, startled, and motions to me to be quiet.

"You're not on your own there, are you?" she asks. "Mmm. Okay, good." She pauses, listening. "I know. But she'll be taken good care of. She's safe there. I'll talk to Sophie and call you in the morning."

I can't follow this; I wonder who she is talking to. Gran has lived alone since Granddad died.

"Mmm-hmm," my mother is saying. "I know. I know. She's going to be okay." She leans back on the pillows. "There's nothing more you can do tonight. Just hang in there. Mmm-hmm…I know, but try not to worry too much. Mmm-hmm… Okay. I'll talk to you tomorrow."

Mom puts the phone down. The soft click sounds loud in the quiet of the dim bedroom. She pats the bed beside her. "Come sit here, honey."

I cross the room and sit on the edge of her bed. "Is it Gran?" I ask. My breath catches oddly in my throat.

My mother shakes her head. She reaches out and puts her arm around my shoulders. "It's Zelia."

"Zelia?"

"She…oh, honey. Apparently she tried to kill herself."

"Tried to…"

Mom pulls me closer to her, and I don't resist.

"That was Lee on the phone," she says. She pulls her comforter over my legs. "She was pretty upset, so I'm not totally clear on what happened, but it sounds like Zelia tried to cut her wrists."

"Is she…will she be okay?"

Mom nods. "She's had stitches, and they're keeping her at the hospital for now. She's still in emergency, but they'll admit her for a psych assessment. You can go in and see her tomorrow."

I stare at her, feeling slow and stupid. The words are barely making sense to me. I keep thinking about the cut I saw on her arm. Had she been thinking about doing this even back then?

Mom lifts my hair off my face and tucks it behind my ears. "Sophie, honey…has Zelia ever talked about suicide?"

"No," I say. I think of that little rhyme she recited, sitting on the sidewalk outside the bookstore: *Guns aren't legal*…I can't remember how it went, but I remember what she said afterward.

There's supposed to be some line in there about razors too. And, clear as if it were yesterday, I can see her tossing her hair back and saying, *If I decided to do it, I'd just do it.*

I look at my mother, and then look away, down at the comforter over our knees. "Not seriously," I say. "I was kind of worried about her, but then we had that fight...I never thought she would do something like this." The comforter blurs into swirls of burgundy. I blink and let fat tears drop onto the bed.

Mom takes my chin in her hand and tilts my face up toward hers. "This isn't your fault, Sophie." She holds my gaze. "People don't try to kill themselves just because they have a fight with their best friend. There must be something else going on."

I nod a couple of times. Mom lets go of my chin and closes her eyes for a moment. When she opens them again, they are wet and shiny.

"Sophie...promise you'll talk to me if you're ever that unhappy?" she whispers.

"I promise," I whisper back. Then I snuggle down under the covers and close my eyes. Mom turns out the light. She lies down beside me, and she keeps her arm around me until I fall asleep.

Twenty-three

WHEN I WAKE up it is morning, and I am alone in my mother's bed. I am disoriented for a second; then it all comes crashing in. I roll over and bury my face in the soft pillows, smell my mother's shampoo. I want to cry, but no tears come.

At some point Mom comes in and says something about school today. I turn my face away and say nothing. All morning I slip in and out of a drowsy unsettled sleep. I dream about Zelia. I dream that we are on a bus riding through the night, and rain is falling on the dark streets outside. Zelia keeps getting up and trying to get off the bus, and it is very important somehow that I persuade her to stay with me.

I guess Mom decided we would both take the day off, because when she comes back it is past noon. She is wearing sweats and carrying a tray with toast, peanut butter and a sliced apple.

She slides a pile of books and academic journals off her bedside table to make room for the tray. "Sophie, honey..."

"Hi, Mom."

She perches on the edge of the bed. "How are you doing?"

"Okay."

"I brought you some lunch," she says, gesturing toward the tray. "Try to eat something."

I'm about to decline automatically, to say I'm not hungry, when I remember Max's eyes locked on mine and her voice saying, *How is that any different from what Zelia is doing?*

"Okay," I say. I really am not hungry, but I eat a little toast anyway and some of the apple.

Mom watches me eat. "Sophie, if you want to go up to the hospital this afternoon…"

I shake my head. "No, I don't."

She studies my face for a minute. Then she stands up. "Okay, honey. I'm just downstairs if you change your mind."

I watch her leave. Then I snuggle back down under the covers and close my eyes. My dream pulls at me strongly; it feels more real than anything else. Maybe if I can convince Zelia to stay on the night bus, everything will be okay when I wake up. Maybe none of this will have happened.

Time drifts by. I'm half awake, half asleep. I don't think about anything, although when the phone rings I wonder if it is Lee.

Sometime later, Mom comes back in. "Sophie, I've run you a bath. I'm going out for a bit. Go get in the tub and have a soak. Then maybe you could come downstairs for a while."

I let Mom help me out of bed. My legs are wobbly and feeble, like I've been sick. In the bathroom, the light is too bright for my eyes. My usually pink-cheeked face looks pale and ugly in the mirror.

Lying in the tub, my mind slowly starts to fill up with thoughts again. Zelia. The shoplifting, her anger, the cut on her arm. The thing with Michael that no one else knows about. Our fight. Me talking to Max about being worried but not doing anything more about it. Zelia. In hospital. I picture her lying in a narrow hospital bed, white sheets pulled up tightly, tubes dripping liquid into her bandaged arms. *For the eyeing of my scars, there is a charge.* I try to remember the rest of that poem, but all I can remember is one other line: *Dying is an art, like everything else.*

Even at the very worst times I have never wanted to die.

I slide down and let my head slip under the water. Warm. Quiet. I can hear my heart beating.

The water is getting cold by the time I finally emerge. I pull on flannel pajama bottoms and a baggy T-shirt and head downstairs. My mother is sitting in the living room with Gran. Anxiety shoots through my body like stray electricity. I had been so scared when I thought something had happened to Gran, but now I just don't feel tough enough to cope with her. I look down at my hands, which are pink from the hot bath. They look how I feel: raw and sort of newborn.

Gran beckons to me. "Sophie, come here." She pats a spot beside her on the couch. "Your mother told me about your friend. Zelia."

I cross the living room slowly and sit down beside her. "Yeah."

She purses her lips tightly and studies my face. "She'll be okay. They always are, that type. They don't give up so easily."

I stiffen. I'm not in the mood to hear criticism of Zelia right now.

Mom notices and tries to come to the rescue. "Sophie, why don't you come in the kitchen with me and help get dinner ready?"

I start to get to my feet but Gran grabs my arm. "Sit down, Sophie." She turns to my mother. "Jeanie, why don't you go in the kitchen and start? I want to talk to Sophie."

Mom's eyes meet mine in a silent apology. "Okay."

Gran turns and looks at me. "Now, don't you be getting your knickers in a knot. I'm not going to pass judgment on your friend."

I look at her, wary but curious.

She doesn't say anything for a moment. I start to fidget uncomfortably. I wish she'd just get on with it.

"I could tell that girl had problems," she says.

"I thought you said you weren't going to pass judgment."

She glares at me. "I'm just stating facts. She was obviously a bad influence."

I roll my eyes. "Are you going to give me a lecture about peer pressure now?"

Gran lifts her chin and looks at me with hard eyes. "Friends have all things in common. That's from Plato, miss. I don't suppose anyone studies the classics anymore, but I suggest you think about it."

I tense up. "You can't blame Zelia for the way I am," I say, glaring right back at her. "I make my own choices, you know."

"Do you now?"

There is a challenge in her voice. I stand up; then I turn and look down at her. "Yeah. I do."

There is a long pause. Finally Gran shakes her head and looks away, like she's giving up on me.

I start to walk away.

"I was a teenager once, you know," she calls after me.

It's such a cliché. I can hardly believe she actually said it. I spin around. "Yeah. A hundred years ago."

She looks right at me. "Do you think anyone ever forgets?"

Her face is neutral, but I feel like she just slapped me. Never, I think. Not in a hundred years.

IN THE KITCHEN, Mom is stirring a pot on the stove. She jumps slightly when I come in. "Don't tell Gran it's not home-made," she says. She rinses the empty cans and drops them into the recycling bin. Then she turns and looks at me. "Everything okay?"

I shrug. "I guess."

"Is Gran giving you a hard time?"

"Just being Gran. You know."

Mom makes a face. "I do know, believe me." She squeezes my shoulder. "She does care about you. And she isn't good at showing it, but she means well."

"Yeah." I don't think meaning well is much use at all, but I don't say anything. I stare at my reflection in the dark window. "I don't want to go to the hospital tonight," I whisper. "I don't want to see her."

Mom stops stirring and turns to look at me. Her forehead is furrowed with concern. "Because of that fight you had?" she asks. "Or are you scared because of what she tried to do?"

I wait for a moment and check around inside to see if I know the answer. My mind stays blank, and I feel empty, hollow and tired. "I don't know."

Mom touches my cheek quickly and so softly I can barely feel it. "Honey…I don't want to put pressure on you…but I think you are probably a lot more important to Zelia than you realize. More important than she lets on." She hesitates. "She must have been feeling pretty desperate to do something like this."

"Do you think it's my fault?" I whisper.

"No, of course it isn't. Like I said before, people don't try to kill themselves just because of a fight with a friend. It's a lot more complicated than that." She ducks her head, trying to get me to meet her eyes. "Would you say it's my fault because I told Zelia to leave after she broke into my files?"

I shake my head. "Of course not."

"Well, okay then. And it's not your fault either."

I blink back tears. "I think I'm going to go back to bed," I say.

Mom pours some soup into a bowl. "Take this up with you," she says. "And, Sophie? Please try to eat it."

Twenty-four

THE NEXT MORNING I get up and go to school as if every-thing is normal. Mom doesn't mention Zelia, though I can tell she is thinking about her. She is softer and quieter than usual, treating me like I am made of glass. I sit through my morning classes in a daze, doodling tiny inky pictures in the margins of my notebooks: horses, girls' faces, the night bus Zelia and I rode in my dream.

At lunchtime, Max meets me at my locker.

"Thought I'd see what you were up to," she says.

"Not much." I want Max to know what's going on, but I don't know quite how to tell her. It sounds so unreal, so melodramatic, to say that Zelia tried to commit suicide. "Max... can we go somewhere to talk?"

"Sure." She frowns. "Are you okay? Stupid question. Again. You're not okay. Obviously." She takes my arm and steers me through the crowded hallway and outside. We walk in silence across the wet field and down into the square.

Max gestures to the empty steps in front of the theater. I sit. She sits beside me, sideways on the step, with her knees pulled up to her chest and her arms wrapped around them. "So," she says.

"So," I say. "So…" I tug at my lower lip with my teeth; then I just blurt it out. "Zelia tried to kill herself."

Max's eyebrows fly upward. "Oh no. Shit. Is she going to be okay?"

I nod. "I guess. She's in hospital."

"What did she do?"

"She cut her wrists." The square is littered with dead leaves. Someone rakes them up early in the morning, and they blow all over the place by lunchtime.

Max gives me a sideways look. "Shit," she says again. "I can't believe this. I mean, I knew you were worried about her, but…"

I make a face and stare at the leaves fluttering across the cobblestones. "I know. I didn't think she'd do something like this."

"You're not blaming yourself, are you?" Max asks.

I shrug. "Yes and no."

"Come on, Sophie. You're way too smart for that."

I grimace. "Not smart enough to see this coming."

We sit in silence for a minute. The cold of the steps is seeping through my jeans. I tuck my hands into my jacket pockets.

"So is that why you weren't in school yesterday? You went to see her?" Max asks.

"How'd you know I wasn't in school?"

Max grins a little sheepishly. "Thought we could hang out. I looked for you at lunchtime."

"Huh." I feel a quick flash of warmth, followed by the guilty realization that a small part of me doesn't want Zelia to come back to school. I don't want to stop spending time with Max. I wish she and Zelia could just get along.

"So—did you?"

I sigh. "No, Mom wanted me to but...I don't know, Max. I just couldn't."

Max stares at me. "What do you mean, you couldn't?"

I can feel my cheeks turning red. "I don't want to see her," I mumble.

"Sophie, you're supposed to be her best friend. She tried to kill herself. You can't just dump her."

My nail polish is gone so I pick at the reddened skin around my cuticle. "I'm not dumping her."

Max continues to stare at me.

"I'm not," I protest. "It's just, I can't, I..."

Max stands up. "Come on," she says.

"What?"

"Come on. I've got the car here. I'll go with you."

I gape at her. "Now? To the hospital?"

"Yup." She holds out a hand to pull me up.

"What about our classes?"

Max snorts. "Please. Don't tell me you haven't skipped for less important things than this."

I remember telling Gran that I make my own choices. Do I? Is this my choice or Max's? I sit there for a long moment until I know the answer. It's my choice. Because Max is right: I'm Zelia's best friend, and she needs me.

I reach out and take Max's outstretched hand. "Okay," I say. "Let's go."

MAX WAITS IN the lobby, and I ride the elevator up to the third floor. The adolescent psychiatric ward is a long hallway, blocked by a reception desk. It isn't what I pictured. There are no obviously crazy people wandering around. It just looks like any other hospital ward.

"I'm here to see Zelia," I say.

The woman behind the desk taps her long pink nails on the shiny counter. "Zelia Keenan? Room three-one-two."

Zelia is sitting cross-legged on her bed, reading a book and looking reassuringly normal. I try to act like I visit friends in the psych ward every day.

"Hey."

She looks up and gives me her lopsided half grin. "Hey."

"Are you, you know, okay?" I ask.

She nods. "Fine. Everyone is totally overreacting."

"They are?"

"Uh-huh. I didn't try to kill myself. God. I'm not crazy."

I nod. I can't help glancing at the white bandage peeking out from under the sleeve of her sweatshirt.

Zelia follows my eyes and shrugs. "I just cut myself sometimes, okay? It's not a big deal. I didn't mean to do it so deep."

I stare at her. There is a strange feeling in my gut, like I'm on an elevator with a broken cable. She is looking at me as if what she said was the most normal thing in the world.

As if everyone just cuts themselves, a little, sometimes.

"You...you cut yourself? On purpose?" I say. "Why?"

Zelia looks away and stares out the window. When she answers, her voice is so soft I can barely hear her. "I don't know," she says.

All at once, I realize that I've only seen what I needed to see in her. Strength, confidence, daring, that way of being so absolutely alive in every moment. All the things I wanted to be. I haven't seen what was really there. I haven't seen how much she must have been hurting. I swallow hard and change the subject quickly. "So...how long are you going to be here?"

"No idea." Zelia leans toward me and drops her voice to a conspiratorial whisper, "It's not that bad, you know. My roomie's cool." She gestures toward the unmade bed across from hers in the narrow room. "She's seventeen and she sings in a band. Dead Valentines. Have you heard of them?"

I shake my head.

Zelia looks disappointed. "Well, me neither actually. But anyway, she wants me to go see them play when we get out of here."

"That's great," I say. I stand beside her bed, feeling awkward. I look down at the magazines I bought in the hospital gift shop. Somehow I had pictured Zelia being more sick, more subdued. She seems just like she always does. Except for the bandages.

"Here," I say, thrusting the magazines toward her.

She glances at them and drops them on the bed. "Thanks." Then she looks at her watch. "Hey, Sophie, I have to go to this group thing in a couple of minutes." She rolls her eyes at me comically.

"It's totally lame. We all have to sit in a circle and compete to see who is the biggest loser."

"What do you say?" I ask curiously. Zelia isn't really the support-group type.

She laughs. "Oh, I have fun. I think today I'll tell them about how my little sister was run over by a fire truck when I was four."

I frown. "You don't have a younger sister."

She laughs again. "Hey, they want me to share, so I share."

I chew on my lower lip. "Zelia...other people are telling real things...you know, true stories. I don't know. It just seems..."

Zelia swings her legs around and jumps off the bed in one fluid motion. "Oh, Sophie, lighten up. You're getting to be no fun at all." She pops a piece of gum in her mouth and snaps it loudly. "Anyway, I have to go. Come see me again, okay?"

And she is gone. I sit on the edge of her bed and stare at the rumpled sheets for a few minutes. Then I get up and take the elevator back downstairs.

Max is waiting in the lobby. "So," she says. "Okay?"

"Okay," I say.

"How was she?"

I make a face. "I don't know. She seemed just like usual. It was weird."

Max waits.

"I don't think she's even going to try to deal with stuff," I say. "She doesn't even seem to think she has a problem."

"Well...I guess everyone has to deal with their own shit." She watches me. "Or not."

I don't think she means it as a challenge, but her words catch and tug at something inside me. I think maybe it's time I started to deal with mine. And I think I'm going to have to start way back at the beginning. To start over and tell the truth this time.

Twenty-five

THE NEXT DAY, after school, I open my drawer and pull out the bag of rings Zelia and I got from the gumball machines at the drugstore. I stuff it into the pocket of my leather jacket and head downstairs.

"Ready to go?" Mom asks.

I nod. We walk out to the car, and she drives me down to the hospital.

Mom parks the car and comes in with me. In the main lobby, she takes my hand and gives it a squeeze.

"Do you want me to go up with you?" she asks.

"No, I'll be okay." I haven't told her that I skipped school to visit Zelia yesterday.

"If you're sure...I'll meet you back down by the coffee shop."

I nod and ride the elevator back up to Zelia's ward.

She is sitting on a couch in a common area, reading a magazine. She looks up and smiles when I walk in.

"Hey, Zelia," I say. I sit down on the couch beside her. Zelia groans when she sees that I have brought her a stack of assignments and notes from missed classes.

"Mr. Farley says not to worry about the due dates—he'll give you extensions—but to try to do the readings if you can," I tell her.

We chat for a while, mostly about school. I tell her I finally handed in my *Lord of the Flies* essay and that Mr. Farley has assigned yet another paper. It is so strange. Here we are in a psychiatric ward, and we are talking like we always do. We could be in her living room. It is so tempting to pretend that everything is normal—that the fight never happened, that she never tried to kill herself, and that there is nothing wrong.

I take a deep breath. "Zelia..." I say slowly, "there's something I haven't told you. About myself, I mean. Something I haven't been totally honest about."

She perks up and leans toward me. "Really? What?"

I bite the inside of my lip. This is harder than I thought it would be. "I want you to know why I'm telling you this." I tilt my head and look at her blue eyes. "So if it...if it changes how you see me or anything..."

Zelia grabs my arm. "Sophie, so mysterious! Let me guess... you've found Jesus? No, no. Too cliché. Let me think..."

I interrupt. "I'm serious."

"Okay, okay." She is pouting now, but I keep going anyway.

"Look, I think part of the reason you are in here is because you don't face up to stuff. I mean, neither of us do. I haven't been dealing with my stuff either."

Zelia's face is still. She watches me warily.

I plow on, not wanting to lose my momentum or my nerve. "Okay. So I want that to change, you know? I want us to be stronger. Both of us."

"Get to the secret," Zelia says.

I sigh. "Okay. Okay. The thing I haven't told you is that back in Georgetown, in grade nine, I was kind of...well, I was... well, you probably would have thought I was an Ermentrude."

She throws her head back and laughs; then she looks at me appreciatively. "Good one, Sophie."

"I'm not kidding," I tell her.

"Oh, come on. This is payback for me telling the support group that my sister got run over by a fire truck, right?"

I shake my head. "No. No, it isn't."

Zelia stares at me. "I don't get it. What do you mean?"

I struggle to find words. "I...I...you would have thought... I mean, the way I dressed and stuff...well, you wouldn't have been my friend back then. And some of the girls were pretty mean. Really mean actually. Worse than they are to Ermentrude Clements."

Zelia shakes her head. "I don't get why you're telling me this."

I clear my throat. I'm starting to feel unsure of this myself. "I just wanted to be honest about it." I can feel tears prickling my eyes and I ignore them, blink hard and continue. "When we moved out here, I tried to change. I wanted to fit in. I was so happy when we became friends. But I feel bad that I kind of, you know, kind of hid who I used to be." I look at her and chew on my lip. "Do you understand?"

She stands up. "I don't think you should go around telling people this, Sophie. I mean, really. Not a good idea to spread that story around."

"I'm just telling you. Zelia. My friend." I hold my breath and touch the bag of rings in my pocket. Are we still friends?

She frowns. "Yeah, well. I just think, it's over, right? Like you said, who you used to be. History."

It would be so easy to just agree, let it go, but something isn't sitting right with me. "Yeah. Yeah. But who I used to be... I mean, it's still there, you know? Still part of who I am."

Zelia sits back down and leans toward me. "What is your point, Sophie? You're saying you want to be part Ermentrude?"

"I'm saying I want to be who I am." I hesitate. "And I guess I'm saying that the things that happen to us don't just go away."

Zelia scowls. "Yeah? In my life, they do. Over. Done. Gone."

I meet her eyes. "Yeah. And look how well that's working for you." I can't believe I said that out loud. I brace myself for her anger.

To my surprise, she just laughs. "Points for that one, Sophie." She looks at me appraisingly. "Anyway, enough of the heavy stuff, okay? Give me some gossip."

I try to switch gears. "Can't think of anything, really." I stick my hands in my pockets and find the bag of rings still there. I've told her my secret, and more than anything I want to hear her say that we're still friends. I want the reassurance of our rituals and games. I start to slide the bag out of my pocket.

"Come on...what's new at school? Hey, what about you and that hottie out at the barn?"

I look at her blankly. "Huh?"

Zelia tosses her hair. "You know. Travis."

"Tavish," I say. I shove the bag of rings back in my pocket, feeling flustered and caught off guard. "I thought you said he was a geek."

She shrugs. "Whatever. Don't tell me you're not into him... you're blushing!"

I know I am. I hate conversations like this. "Nothing to tell," I say.

"Ohhhh...Come on. Your face is bright red. You've got the hots for him, admit it." Zelia is laughing, playing with me like a cat with a mouse.

I try to think of how some other girl might respond. "He's not my type," I say, doing my best to sound casual.

Zelia leans toward me. "Who is, then?" she asks. "Who is your type?"

I shrug.

She narrows her eyes. "Max?"

I stare at her. "What?"

"Come on. She's such a dyke."

"She's not," I say hotly. "You just don't like her."

"True," Zelia says. Tah-rue. "I don't like her much. But she's still a dyke."

My thoughts are slow and thick. "Why do...I mean... she had...I don't..."

Zelia looks at me scornfully. "If you don't know, you're like the only person who doesn't. I heard she was actually going out with a girl from some other school."

I remember Max mentioning her ex, saying he went to a different school. Had she actually said *he*? Or had I just assumed that?

I shake my head, as if I can shake off these thoughts, as if I can shake off these feelings like a dog shaking off water. "I have to go," I say. "Mom's waiting for me downstairs."

Zelia raises one eyebrow and laughs. "Who's running away from things now?"

Twenty-six

BACK AT HOME, I lie on the couch, half studying, half daydreaming. Mom is sitting beside me, folding a pile of laundry into the plastic hamper.

"How are you doing?" she asks.

I hesitate. "Okay, I guess."

She flicks aside a stray lock of hair that has escaped from her ponytail. "You and Zelia aren't getting along so well, are you?"

I make a face and pick up a towel, still warm from the dryer. "No, but she's in hospital. I mean, she's not exactly having a good time, is she?"

Mom tilts her head to one side. "You're not feeling responsible for her, I hope."

I fold the towel lengthwise, and then in thirds. "No, but I don't want to bail on her, either."

"Of course you don't," Mom says. "You're a good friend. I just hope she knows it."

I look at her questioningly. "What do you mean?"

"I hope she appreciates you." She looks as though she wants

to say more. Then she just reaches over and ruffles my hair. "I should let you study."

I drop my eyes back to the page of my notebook. So far, all I have done is draw a row of tiny horses, galloping and jumping through the algebraic equations.

ZELIA CALLS JUST as I am getting into bed.

"They say I can go home in a few days," she says.

I slip under the covers and stretch out. "That's great. Are you, you know…how are you doing?"

"Okay. But I was wondering…I don't know if Lee is going to want me to come home. And Michael…I don't think I want to see him."

This is the first time she has mentioned his name since the day of our big fight. I take the opening and ask carefully, "Did something else happen with him? After we talked? Is that why you…cut yourself?"

There is a long silence on the other end of the phone. I picture Zelia standing at the pay phone in the hospital's windowless hallway. I can hear her breathing.

"He just ignored me," she says softly. "Totally, like I wasn't even there."

"What about the earrings?"

Another silence. "An apology. He said they were an apology. That he shouldn't have kissed me."

"Well, he shouldn't have." I don't know how to make sense of whatever happened with Michael. When it comes to Zelia's stories, sometimes it's hard to know exactly what the truth is. All I know is that she's hurt, and maybe that's all that really matters. "Maybe he realized that he did something wrong," I say slowly. "The earrings…and even ignoring you… maybe he was just trying to make it right again somehow."

Zelia's voice is so soft I can barely hear it. "But I feel so… I don't want to be there, with him."

"Do you want to come here?" I ask slowly.

"Do you think your mom would let me?"

I pause. I still feel angry and confused. I can't stop thinking about what she said about Max. "I don't know," I say. "I can ask."

MOM IS IN bed but her light is on, so I knock softly.

"Mom? I just got off the phone with Zelia. She's getting out of hospital this weekend. She wants to know…can she come here?"

She puts down her book. "Sophie, you know she can't."

I feel an unexpected rush of relief. "I know."

Mom pats the bed, and I cross the room to sit down beside her.

"Aren't you worried about her?" I ask.

Mom nods and sighs. "I've talked to Lee," she admits. "I think she and Zelia really need to get things sorted out between them. Zelia can visit, of course. She can come here to see you, but I'm not sure that letting her stay here would help her and Lee in the long run."

"So Lee does want her to come home then? Zelia wasn't sure."

"Of course she does. She's nervous about it—she doesn't always know how to handle Zelia—but she wants her to come home."

"What about Michael?"

Mom hesitates. "Don't say anything to Zelia. Lee is going to tell her tomorrow. It's over. He's going to be moving out this weekend."

I grin. "That'll make Zelia happy, anyway."

"And it'll mean Lee can focus on her daughter. I think Zelia needs that."

I raise my eyebrows. "Do you think she will? Lee, I mean? Do you think she'll put Zelia first?"

She sighs. "Oh, Sophie. I don't know. I think this suicide attempt really scared her. I think she'll do her best. And I guess…well, that's all any of us can do."

I look down at my hands. "You know, I felt like I had to ask if she could stay here, but, well, it's okay that you said no."

Mom pulls me close and gives me a quick hug. "I do love you, Sophie Keller. You know that, don't you?"

I nod and squirm away, pleased but embarrassed. "You too, Mom."

"Sophie…"

"Yeah?"

She looks uncomfortable. "All this stuff with Zelia and Lee and Michael…I've been wanting to talk to you about something." She hesitates. "It's just that, well…if I was to start seeing someone, I hope you know that I'll always have time for you too. You wouldn't be any less important to me." She rests her hand on my arm briefly. "You do know that, don't you?"

I look at her, startled. "Patrick?"

Mom's cheeks are pink, and I realize she blushes as easily as I do. "Maybe," she says. "I think so."

I think about that for a moment. ",Well," I say. "Well."

She laughs. "Can I take that to mean you can handle the idea of your mom going out on a date or two?"

"I guess so," I say. She hasn't dated anyone for years, and it's pretty weird to imagine someone being in her life—in our lives—in that way. To be honest, I'd rather no one was, but I guess that's not really fair. And if she has to date someone, Patrick seems all right. I shrug. "Yeah," I say. "It's okay."

AT SCHOOL THE next day, I keep thinking about what Zelia said about Max. *She's such a dyke.* I remember that time in my room when Max said she wanted to tell me something and then changed her mind.

My math text lies open on my desk: *A cubic meter of water weighs 1000 kilograms. What is the weight of a waterbed mattress that is 2 meters by 3 meters by 20 centimetres if the casing of the mattress weighs 1 kilogram?* I doodle on the edge of the page and try to sort out what I am feeling. Curiosity about whether it is true. Hurt that she didn't tell me. And there's something else too, something I have been trying not to think about: those words scrawled on my locker last year. *Sophie Keller is a dyke.*

At lunchtime, Max is waiting for me. Despite everything, I can't stop a smile sneaking across my face when I see her.

"Hey," I say. I feel suddenly shy.

Max grins at me. "Hey yourself." She picks up her backpack and slings it over one shoulder. "So guess what? Mom let me have the car today, so I can ride after school. Anyway, I thought we could take our lunches and drive somewhere. If you want."

I nod. "Okay. Sure. It'd be good to get away from school. I don't really want to be here today."

We decide to go to Beacon Hill Park, but it starts raining just before we arrive. Max keeps driving, right past the park and down to the cliffs at Dallas Road. We sit in the parked car and watch the waves crashing on the shore.

Max unwraps her sandwich. "Some picnic," she says glumly. "I hope it stops raining before tonight. I was supposed to go for a ride with Tavish."

"Uh-huh," I say, half listening. The wind is picking up, blowing ferociously. During the stronger gusts I can feel the car moving slightly. The rain is coming down in hard diagonal sheets, sluicing down the windshield and bouncing off the hood like hail.

Max looks at me apprehensively. "You *are* going to eat something, right?"

I nod, pull an apple out of my pocket and turn it in my hands. "Uh-huh."

It's weird. Even after seeing those old pictures of myself, even after realizing I was never fat after all—even after deciding that I had to deal with all this stuff—eating is still hard.

I take a bite of apple and chew. It tastes like nothing.

I look at Max. My stomach is in knots. I wonder if anything will change between us if I ask her about what Zelia said.

She frowns. "Is something wrong? You're so quiet."

"I, uh, Max. There's something...Zelia said something about you. I don't know if it's true but..."

"What did she say?"

"She said you were...that you are...gay."

Max just looks at me. Motionless. Waiting.

I turn in my seat to face her. "I don't care if you are. I mean, I care but I don't...you know..."

Max is quiet for a moment, and I listen to the drumming of the rain on the car roof. Her eyebrows are drawn down, straight dark lines over her brown eyes. A muscle twitches in her jaw. "I'm sorry," she says. "I should've told you the truth."

"It's not like you lied to me," I say. I'm trying not to feel hurt that she didn't trust me. "I just...I guess I just made an assumption."

"I lied," Max says. Her eyes are dry but her voice is low and full of tears. "There are lots of ways to lie. I just lied with silence instead of words."

I'm quiet for a few minutes, thinking. Lying with silence. That's the same thing I've been doing ever since I left Georgetown. "It's okay," I say. "Really. I get it."

"You know, I really wanted to tell you," Max says. "I didn't want you to find out from someone else."

"Why didn't you?"

She sighs, looks at me quickly and looks away again. "I wasn't sure how you'd react. Not that I thought you'd be homophobic.

I know you're not like that. I just didn't want you to be uncomfortable around me."

"I wouldn't have been."

Max shrugs. "Lots of girls would. Jas and Maisie are. Not that they'll admit it." She scowls. "You'll notice they don't necessarily want to hang out with me anymore, though."

I study her face. "They just say you're really busy. Doing your own thing. They've never said anything bad about you."

"No?"

"No. Actually, I got the impression that they thought you didn't have time for them."

Max doesn't say anything for a moment. Then she sighs. "I don't know. Maybe I'm paranoid. To be fair, I guess I haven't given them much of a chance to get used to the idea."

The wind and rain are deafening. I shiver and pull my jacket tighter around me. Max starts the engine and cranks the heat.

"Max?"

"Yeah."

"Can I ask you something? It's kind of personal."

She looks at me warily. "I guess so."

I think for a moment. "I just wondered…how do you know you're gay?" I'm worried about using the wrong words, worried about her thinking I'm judging or doubting her. "I don't mean I don't believe you. I just mean, how did you decide? I mean, did you always know or…"

Max runs her hands through her spiky hair and lets them drop back onto the steering wheel. "I think I've always known."

She pauses, looking thoughtful. "Last year I tried dating a guy. It didn't last long. It just felt all wrong." She turns to me. "Actually, don't mention this to anyone, but it was Tavish."

"Really?" For some reason, this bothers me a little.

"Yeah. But like I said, it didn't go anywhere. We're good friends, but that's where we should have left it. But that's okay. He's a cool guy, and we're still buddies."

"Huh." I stare out the window, squint into the rain, watch the waves sending sheets of salty spray high into the air.

Max gives me a crooked grin. "I figured if I couldn't feel that way for a guy like Tavish, I might as well quit trying."

I nod, trying to take this all in, to figure out where it all fits, where I fit. I should have known that Max, always so sure of herself, would be sure about this too.

"Max?"

"Yeah."

"You know how I told you about the stuff that happened back at my old school? The stuff those girls did?"

She nods.

I roll the words around in my mouth, trying to feel out how they will sound. "They wrote on my locker one time. They wrote...they wrote *Sophie Keller is a dyke.*"

Max's face looks all tight, like she's thinking a whole bunch of things and trying to decide which ones to say out loud. Finally she just looks at me and shrugs. "Assholes."

"Yeah. Yeah, but..."

She shakes her head. "But nothing. They're assholes. Anyway, it's something only you can know."

I make a face. "But I don't know."

We sit in silence for a minute. Max sighs.

"Look," she says. "This is the way I see it, okay? I think... some people just always know. Like me. And then a whole lot of people never even think about it. They just assume they're straight and they never even question it. And then, for some people, it's just not that clear."

I stare at her. "That's it? I thought you were going to tell me something helpful."

Max laughs softly. "I'm sorry. But you'll figure it all out, Soph. You're one of the smartest people I know." She grins at me. "Well, most of the time, anyway."

"Thanks a lot," I say. I haven't figured anything out, but for some reason I feel a little better. Like maybe not knowing isn't really such a problem after all.

Twenty-seven

ON SATURDAY MORNING, I sleep late and wake up to a blue sky and sunlight streaming in my window. There is frost on the grass, as if winter arrived overnight.

I throw off the covers, pull on jeans and a sweatshirt, and splash water on my face. In the mirror, my gray eyes look wide and startled and my hair is a wild frizzy mess. I take the stairs two at a time. I have to remind myself to eat. Force myself, really. Breakfast, lunch, dinner. Sometimes I manage it, and sometimes I don't. Even so, it feels like an absurd amount of food after months of starving myself. And I am still nervous about gaining weight.

I pour myself a bowl of cereal. Max says I'm way too skinny. I know she's right, sort of. I can see it every time I look in the mirror now. Still, it's helpful to have her as a more neutral observer. I don't always trust myself, but I do trust her to tell me the truth. So I'm trying to keep eating, at least a little. It feels scary, but okay. It feels like I'm in control.

MOM DRIVES ME to the hospital. She's had her hair high-lighted with blond streaky bits, and she keeps checking it out in the rearview mirror.

"It looks good," I say.

She looks at me. "Do you think so? Not too obvious? Not too much?"

"No, it's nice. It looks like summer. Like you've been at the beach."

She adjusts the mirror back to its proper position and turns in to the hospital entrance. "Here we are." She pulls up to the passenger drop-off area and stops the car. Then she turns off the engine. "Sophie…"

"Yeah?"

"Look, I know you're probably in a rush to see Zelia, but there never seems to be a good time to talk lately. And I just wanted to say something."

I feel instantly anxious, like I've done something wrong.

Mom looks as nervous as I feel. "This move out to Victoria," she begins, "it's been a lot harder than I thought it would be. Seeing your Gran all the time…well, I've been thinking a lot about what it was like when I was growing up."

"You have?" It's so hard to imagine Mom being my age, although obviously I know she was.

She pulls on her lower lip with her teeth, just like I do when I'm nervous. "I love my mother. You know that. I wouldn't have moved us out here if I didn't."

"Of course, I know that." I look at her, wondering where she is going with this.

She sighs. "The thing is, Gran used to nag at me constantly. She criticized every little thing I did. Everything. And she always had a million questions about where I was going and who I was seeing."

"I can imagine," I say, feeling a surge of sympathy at the thought of having Gran for a mother.

"I feel bad saying that about her, but I want you to understand. I've always promised myself I wouldn't be like her, as a mother. I don't want to…well, be on your case, as you'd say."

I shake my head. "You're not."

She looks at me for a minute without saying anything. "Well, good. I'm glad you don't think so. But I have been worried about you since we moved out here, and I don't know…I wanted to respect your privacy, but maybe I should have asked more questions about what was going on."

"Mom…I like it here. Better than Georgetown." I meet her eyes. "Honest."

"Good. Good. But I just wanted to say, if you ever want to talk to me about anything…"

"No, I don't. I mean, I don't need to. I'm fine."

She nods. "I'm glad. But you know, if you weren't fine… and you didn't want to talk to me…there are other people you could talk to."

I turn away and look out the window at the hospital. "You mean, like counselors?"

"Uh-huh."

"I don't need that," I say quickly.

She nods again. "That's fine. I just wanted to make sure you knew it was an option."

I don't say anything for a minute. I think I might cry if I try to talk, and I don't want to. I swallow hard. "Mom."

"Sophie."

"I know I can talk to you."

"Good." She smiles at me, but her eyes are serious. "But believe me, I know that sometimes it's easier to talk to someone who isn't your mother."

I shake my head. "You're not like Gran."

Mom sighs. "Oh, I try not to be. But sometimes…well."

A car honks behind us.

"Damn it," Mom says. She sticks her hand out the window and waves for the car to go around us. "I guess you'd better go."

"Okay." I don't move. "Mom?"

"What is it?"

I shrug. "I don't know. Just, thanks."

She smiles. "Say hi to Zelia for me. I hope she's doing better."

"I will."

The car honks again, the driver leaning on the horn this time. Mom and I exchange glances.

"Type A driver," she says. "You'd better go."

"At least if he has a stroke, he's already at the hospital."

Mom shakes her head at me, but we're both laughing as I get out of the car and wave good-bye.

I RIDE THE elevator up to Zelia's ward. I still have to tell her that she can't stay with us and I wonder how she'll react. Zelia's unpredictability used to draw me to her. Now it worries me. I don't want to lose her, but I don't know if she'll let things be different between us. She's always been the one who makes the rules.

Zelia's allowed to go out for a walk with me, so we wander through the hospital grounds and over to the Starbucks by the grocery store. I order a black coffee for myself and a chai latte for her, and we sit at a table by the window. It seems like we should be able to feel the warmth of the sun, but people keep coming in and out and the draft is icy.

She's in a good mood, chattering away about the other patients she has met and the staff on the ward. Her stories are awfully funny and I can't help laughing, even though sometimes I think I shouldn't.

Finally she asks, "So did you ask your mom?"

I nod.

Zelia looks at me. Some emotion I can't identify flickers across her face and she lifts her chin. "I guess she said no, huh?"

"Yeah." I hesitate and take a sip of my coffee. It is tempting just to let my mother take the blame.

She gives me a lopsided grin. "I knew she was going to. She came to see me."

I almost spill my drink. "She did?"

"Yeah. She didn't tell you?"

I shake my head.

"Right after—you know. The next day."

"Before me," I say. I know when it must have been: when I was lying in the tub feeling sorry for myself.

Zelia meets my eyes. "Yeah."

"Zelia…I'm sorry. I should've come sooner."

She shrugs it off. "Whatever."

Her voice cracks a little, and I remember Mom saying that I'm more important to Zelia than I realize.

"I really am sorry," I say. "I got kind of freaked out. Scared." I touch her arm for a second. "I'm glad Mom came."

"Yeah. She was pretty nice to me. But she did say that I couldn't stay with you guys. She thinks Lee and I need to sort things out."

I think about that for a minute. "Will you? Are you going to talk to her?"

Zelia frowns. "Maybe. If she'll listen."

"You know," I say slowly, "I used to think you hung out with me because you liked my mom so much." I wait, watching her face.

She laughs. "Idiot. Your mom is amazing, but I wouldn't hang out with you if I didn't like you."

I let out a long breath. "Well, good."

Zelia laces her fingers together and rests them on the table. "I liked you the first time I saw you. All that gorgeous crazy red hair. You looked like you should be laughing, but you had such a serious face all the time. You were hanging out with those girls. You know, the Clones."

"Yeah?"

"And you looked…I don't know. Bored. Kind of disconnected

or something." She shrugs. "You looked how I always felt."

"Really? I did?" It's the last thing I expected to hear.

Zelia shrugs, looking uncomfortable. As if she's said too much. "Well, whatever. And then when I met your mom, I just thought you were so fucking lucky. If my mom was like that, I'd tell her everything."

"It's not that easy," I say, thinking about the conversation I just had with my mother.

"You don't even try."

I shake my head. She might be right, but I can't take any more in right now. Besides, I think things with Mom and me are changing, maybe. "So you're not mad at her for saying you can't stay with us?"

"Nah." She flips her hair off her face. "I fucked up, with the files and everything. I'm not a total idiot, you know. I get it."

I bite my lip, wondering whether to say anything. Then I take a deep breath and go ahead. "Maybe it's better that way for us too. You know, if you're not staying with us. I mean, I still want to hang out with you, but I want to have other friends too."

Zelia pushes her latte away from her and leans back. Her eyes narrow. "This is about Max, isn't it?"

"Partly," I admit. "I don't want to have to choose between you all the time."

"She really is a dyke, you know. I didn't make that up." There is a spiteful edge to her voice.

I look at her straight on. "I know she's gay. Lesbian. Queer. Whatever. I don't care, Zelia." I don't want to have this conversation now, but there is no way not to.

Zelia looks down and stirs the foamy surface of her drink with her fingertip. "God, don't tell me you're a dyke too."

I am silent for a moment. My heart is beating so fast I wonder if she can hear it. I stick my hands in my jacket pockets. Our bag of rings is still there. "No. Well, I don't know." I shake my head, as if I can shake all the doubts right out of it. "Right now I'm not really interested in getting involved with anybody. At all. And Max and I are just friends, if that's what you're really asking."

Zelia nods but doesn't look up. Her long dark lashes hide her eyes. For a second I wonder if she is crying. Suddenly I realize that Zelia only pretends not to care what other people think. And I totally fell for it because I wanted to be more like that myself.

"I still want to be your friend," I say.

She snaps her head up, chin set. "I don't need your pity. Even if I am…what was it you said? Messed up?"

"I'm sorry I said that," I admit. "I was angry. Anyway, who isn't messed up?"

She looks at me. She has no makeup on, and in the bright sunlight I can see that her blue eyes are ringed with violet shadows. She sighs. "No, it's okay. You were right anyway."

"It's not pity," I say. "I like being with you. I…well, you're really important to me." I reach out my hand and lay it on the table in front of her. "So…are we still friends?"

Zelia takes my hand. "Yeah," she says. "We're still friends."

A grin spreads across my face, and I don't try to hide it. I reach into my pocket with my free hand, pull out the bag of rings and drop it on the table between us.

She grins back. "You know, I had to take out that belly button ring," she says. "It got all infected."

I wince. "Gross."

Zelia turns the bag upside down and the rings tumble out. "You pick first," she says.

I gaze at the jumbled pile of gold, the colored glass glinting blue, red and green. I pick a twisted gold band with a blue stone and slide it onto my finger. It slips down my finger and catches the light.

Zelia picks a matching band with a red stone. She holds up her hand and I hold up mine. Fingertips press to fingertips.

"Friends forever," I say.

Zelia nods slowly. "Friends forever."

Twenty-eight

DECEMBER FLIES BY, cold and clear. Things gradually resume some kind of rhythm. Michael has moved out, and Zelia is back at home with Lee. They seem to be managing. Whenever I ask Zelia how it's going with her mother, she just shrugs and says it's fine. I think maybe it really is.

I know they're seeing a counselor the hospital referred them to. Her name is Julie. Zelia mentions her quite a bit. Julie says this. Julie thinks that.

I tease her about it. "Julie, Julie, Julie. Do I get the impression that you're not absolutely hating talking to this therapist of yours?"

Zelia takes my question seriously. "You know," she says thoughtfully, "I never thought I'd say this, but she's okay." She lifts her chin, flips her hair back over her shoulder and grins. "Not as good as you, Dr. Keller."

I toss my backpack at her. "Goof."

I suspect that Max and Zelia still don't like each other too much, but we don't talk about it and they are at least polite to each other, if not exactly friendly. It would be great if they got along better, but I don't think that's going to happen. Anyway, it's working out okay. I ride with Max and sometimes with Tavish, and I spend most of my lunch hours with Zelia. At least once a week, though, I have lunch with Max.

We go to the pizza place sometimes, or we take our sandwiches and drive down to Dallas Road. If it's cold and windy, we eat in her car, watching the waves crashing and tossing driftwood high onto the beach. One calm sunny day we walk the path winding along the cliff top.

"It's beautiful," Max says. We stop walking and stand facing the water. The mountains are a jagged snow-peaked line against a clear blue sky. A huge container ship looks like a tiny toy against the dark blue water. Bright yellow and green rectangles soar from the cliff: paragliders catching the updraft and flying with the breeze. I draw a deep breath, feel the sun on my face and drink it all in. Something is stirring in my belly, rushing through my veins. I feel like I could fly.

FINALLY SCHOOL BREAKS for the holidays. Patrick is away for a few weeks, visiting his parents in Alberta, but Gran is at our house most days. It's her first Christmas since my grandfather died, and she's finding it hard. She bakes hundreds of cookies; writes Christmas cards; makes red, white and green cross-stitched decorations and hangs them all over the house: stars, snowmen, Christmas trees. I can barely take a step without bumping into them. It's like she's trying to fill every last empty space. Sometimes I sit and help her, threading needles and listening to her talk.

"It's a funny thing," she says one day. "You start thinking your life is complete, polished, everything just the way you want it. And then it all goes and changes on you. Your grandfather dying, you and your mom moving out here...everything is so different."

I pick up a piece of fabric she has dropped and lay it on the table.

She sighs. "I had no idea a year ago that I'd be spending this Christmas with you and Jeanie." She looks at me. "I'm not complaining, mind you. I've never been one to complain about my life."

"That's okay," I say.

Gran picks up the scrap of fabric and turns it in her hands. "I suppose I should make another quilt," she says. "All these little pieces of cloth. Might as well make something from them."

It's hard to imagine that all these odds and ends could be stitched together into something beautiful. "Teach me how," I say impulsively. "Maybe I can help with this one."

Gran actually smiles at me for once. "Maybe you can."

SATURDAY, DECEMBER 21, is Zelia's birthday. It is winter solstice, the shortest darkest day of the year. I love this day. You know that this is as bad as it's going to get and that from here on it will get lighter and brighter as we get closer and closer to spring. It is my first winter in Victoria, and Max has told me that the crocuses will start to come up in January.

I have invited Zelia to come out to the barn today. I call Tavish to ask if she can ride Bug.

"No problem," he says. I can almost hear his wide grin over the phone. "It'll do him good to get out. I don't have time to ride him as much as I should anyway."

"Great. That's great. She'll like that."

"So…is she doing okay, do you think?"

I nod; then I realize he can't see me. "Yeah. I think so."

"Good. I'm glad you're bringing her riding. It'll be good for her as well as Bug."

I laugh. "Equine therapy."

"Exactly," Tavish says.

I'm about to say good-bye but I find myself saying something else. "Tavish? Are you still in touch with friends from Georgetown?" Even as I say the words, I realize something: I'm not scared of the answer. It doesn't matter anymore.

He laughs. "No, we left there when I was twelve. Anyway, to tell you the truth, I didn't really have a lot of friends there."

"You didn't?"

"Nah. Twelve-year-old boys are supposed to play hockey or baseball, not ride horses. Those weren't actually the best years. To be honest, I was pretty happy to leave."

I clear my throat. "Yeah," I say. "Me too. Me too." Someday, I think, Tavish and I might talk about Georgetown.

LEE DROPS ZELIA off at my place in the morning. After lunch, Max picks us up, and we drive out to the barn. Tavish has already brought our horses in from the field and knocked the worst of the mud off for us. Max calls him a sweetie, and I feel a tiny pang of something like jealousy. Lately I have been thinking I am maybe, perhaps, just a little bit in love with them both. It doesn't matter, not yet anyway. Just having friends and being liked for who I am feels like enough of a miracle for now.

We groom, tack up and head out to the woods.

Zelia is riding up front with Tavish. Bug's round belly sways from side to side, and he jogs along to keep up with Schooner's long strides. Max rides beside me; Sebastian and Keltie are more evenly matched.

Max holds her reins in one hand and runs the other through Sebastian's short gray mane. "It's winter solstice," she says.

"I know." I'm surprised. It's not something most people pay attention to.

She grins. "It was some fall, huh."

"Some fall," I agree. We ride in silence for a while, and I think back over the last few months.

"Hey, Max."

"Yeah?"

"Remember that thing I told you about Michelangelo and the sculptures?"

She nods. "Yeah."

"I think I just figured out what's wrong with it."

She looks at me, waiting.

"Well, it's kind of what you said, I guess. About making choices. But also…well, we're never done, are we? I mean, we're always still…"

She nods again. "Changing."

"Yeah." I think about it for a minute. "You know, Mom's dating someone."

Max raises her eyebrows. "And?"

I shrug. "It's weird but okay, I guess." Keltie snorts, as if she's agreeing, and I laugh. "And you won't believe this, but Gran's teaching me how to quilt."

"Your gran? Seriously?"

"Yeah. She's being a bit nicer lately, actually." I picture Gran sitting at the table, surrounded by scraps of cloth and talking about her memories. I have an idea, but I'm not sure I can put it in words quite well enough to say it out loud. This is it: that maybe life is kind of like quilting. That maybe every scrap— every experience—has a place. Maybe nothing needs to be hidden or thrown away.

"Max," I say impulsively, "I'm so glad we're friends."

She raises her eyebrows and grins, her brown eyes locked on mine in a way that makes it hard to look away. "Me too," she says. "Me too."

Just then, Sebastian snorts and leaps to one side. Max quickly puts her free hand on the reins and mutters something softly to him. He is seeing one of his ghosts and is not listening. He snorts, rears up and swings around. His hindquarters barge into Keltie, who squeals indignantly and then leaps sideways.

Next thing I know, I am flat on my back in the mud. Three pairs of eyes are looking down at me. Summer blue, autumn brown, spring green. Zelia, Max and Tavish. They have all dismounted and are standing around me looking anxious.

I give them a feeble grin and struggle to lift my head. "I'm okay."

Max and Zelia reach down to help me up. Tavish has caught Keltie and is stroking her neck soothingly.

"Thanks," I say, taking Zelia's and Max's hands and letting them pull me to my feet. My left leg, hip and back are covered in mud, but I don't seem to be hurt. I move my limbs experimentally. Everything still works.

"You all right?" Zelia asks.

"I'm fine." I shake my head gingerly. "Not quite sure what happened." I take Keltie's reins from Tavish. He doesn't say anything but under the brim of his riding hat, his eyes meet mine with sympathy and humor. He grins at me, and then he turns and places his foot in the stirrup. In one smooth motion, he swings himself back onto his horse.

Zelia is pale. She looks more shaken than me. "God, Sophie. I thought you'd be killed. That looked awful."

Max laughs, not unkindly. "They say it takes a hundred falls before you can call yourself a rider."

"I'd rather just stay a beginner then," Zelia says.

Max laughs again. "Need a leg back up, Sophie?"

I place my muddy boot in her cupped hands and she boosts me up into the saddle. "Thanks."

"No problem." Max looks at her hands ruefully before wiping them off on her black suede chaps. "How about you, Zelia?"

Zelia still looks a little pale, but she shakes her head. "I know how to mount," she says.

Max shrugs. "Whatever you want, birthday girl."

I grin at Max, who manages not to roll her eyes.

Zelia springs gracefully into the saddle, and we ride on down the path, sometimes four abreast, sometimes in single file on the narrow parts. When we come to a place where the trail forks, I call up to the others.

"I'm going to ride the loop trail down along the lakeshore. Let Keltie have a little gallop," I say. "I'll catch up with you in a few minutes."

They nod. I turn off to the right and watch them disappear into the trees. Then it is just Keltie and me. I run my hand down her silky neck. "Ready to go?" I whisper.

I lean forward slightly, press my legs to her sides and open my fingers on the reins as Keltie eases into a gentle canter. Her hooves pound the rhythm of my heartbeat into the solid ground beneath us. I sink my weight down into my heels, tuck my body closer to hers and let her go—faster, faster. Spreading my wings. Flying.

When we reach the lake, Keltie and I finally pull up to a trot and then a walk. The trees are still and solid, dark silhouettes against a blue winter sky. The lake glistens in the sunlight. I jump down lightly and stand at Keltie's side, holding her reins.

I lean against Keltie for a moment, feeling her warmth. I watch our reflection shimmer in the glassy surface of the lake and run my right hand over my left arm, up to my shoulder. The bones at the back are still there but maybe not quite as sharp as they were. I don't need them to be. I'm not running away from the old Sophie Keller anymore. I can feel the muscles moving beneath my sweater, right in that place where I used to imagine wings should grow.

On impulse I bend down and pick up a stone from the water's edge. It is smooth and round in my hand. I throw it as far as I can into the lake and watch it drop through the smooth surface. It barely makes a splash, but its ripples go on forever.